Niyah Moore

Major Jazz

A NOVEL

Giving Your Soul a Rise...One Page at a Time

ISBN- 978-0-9850763-3-7

MAJOR JAZZ by Niyah Moore © 2013

Peace In The Storm Publishing, LLC.
P.O. Box 1152
Pocono Summit, PA 18346

Visit our Web site at www.PeaceInTheStormPublishing.com

MAJOR JAZZ

A NOVEL BY
NIYAH MOORE

Peace In The Storm Publishing, LLC

ACKNOWLEDGEMENTS

First, I would like to thank Jehovah, God, for allowing me to see yet another day. Without him, I wouldn't be. God can work peace through us only if He has worked peace in us. Without God, one can never find peace. I thank Him for peace.

My twelve year old son, Cameron, and nine year old daughter, Ciera, are my blessings. I thank them for being the best kids on the planet. I can't express that enough. We had such a beautiful summer living in the Fillmore. They were definitely a part of this process. To my baby that is an angel in heaven, Londyn, mommy's love is infinite.

My parents, Sharon and Chris Richards, you two keep me going all year, boy, I tell you, but I love you no matter what is going on. No matter what has been done or said, one fact remains the same; I am your child and you are my parents. Enough said.

To Koko, Chris, Kason, David, and Joi, you guys are my family and what keeps me going a lot of times. Without you, I just wouldn't be able to function at times.

I want to thank my publicist, Krishtian Xavier, for bending over backwards to get the Reading Is Sexy Campaign started amongst niyahmoore.com and everything else on the list that needed to be done to make this happen. You are amazing and I am so blessed to have you. Not just

MAJOR JAZZ

saying that because we're family either, I truly am blessed to have you.

Peace in the Storm Publishing, yeah baby, you ladies and gent are my new family. Thank you for embracing me and making me feel so welcome. What an amazing group of talented writers that have so many other talents. We're shining! Thank you Elissa Gabrielle for seeing something in me and believing in my craft. Thank you for bringing *Major Jazz* to life. Our bond is one that I haven't been able to shake ever since that night in Harlem 2011. This year and many more to come, I look forward to our journey. I'm home.

To my beautifully gifted editor, Sharon D Denny, girl, you rocked this thang! I love you for being who you are and sharing your gift with me. My pages sing because of you. I'm honored to be on the same roster as you at Peace in the Storm.

My pen twin, Carla Pennington, you and I are glued FOREVER. We shall link up really soon. It's overdue. No one can have a conversation and laugh so hard like us. You crack me up every single day.

To my handsome co-author of the Pillow Talk Duets, Mr. Stacey L. Moor, it has been so amazing. I look forward to many more projects that may come our way in the future. We have to leave them wanting Moor(e) and we have to give them what they want… so… chop chop!

Frances, Nina, Maya, Myisha, Atija, and Danielle, my sisters, my friends, since high school we have rocked pretty tough in a beautiful way. Ups downs, sideways, and everything else in between, now that cheerleading days are long over, we are raising our beautiful families and friendship seems to be something that will never go away. I love you guys. Tisheena, thank you for always smiling and being so warm. I'm really glad that you and I have become friends as well. You're my girl.

Takia Meacham, girl you are truly supreme. Thank you for gracing my Reading is Sexy photo series. Your professionalism is at the top of the list. We aren't done, so I know you'll be ready.

Tanera Lashaye Daye, thank you for allowing me to spend ten months in Fillmore with you. Without you, I wouldn't have been able to get the research done for this book.

Dario Smith, thank you for supporting my visions as always. Your pictures are always so dope.

My host of friends, cousins, aunts, uncles, and more, it's far too many to name. I love you ALL nonetheless. Please don't kill me for not naming every single one of you.

To my male friends, Scott Gardner, Jonathan Frazier, Julian Johnson, Peyton Watkins, and Paris Moore, you guys truly are great friends. To yet another year of greatness.

MAJOR JAZZ

A very special special special thanks to the authors that have reached out to me this year and have become my mentors in some way shape or form. Karen E. Quinones Miller, it was finally so good to see you this year after seven years! Won't be the last! Eric Jerome Dickey, oh my, yet again, we got to be face to face and I just had to make sure all my books were signed. Don't kill me. LOL. Your girl from Sac needs to be able to see you again. Carl Weber, thank you for the two-hour one on one session inside of Marcus Books, San Francisco. That night is one I shall never forget. Your wisdom and insight truly helped. Mary B. Morrison, thank you for extending your politeness, the phone calls, the radio show, and the referrals, you are such a sweetie. Hope to catch you in Oakland soon. Zane, thank you for personally choosing my vampire short to bless Busy Bodies. The feeling I got when I heard the news made me jump for joy. K'wan, thank you for noticing my aura in Harlem. I try to be warm and friendly to everyone. You are definitely a jewel in the writing business. I respect your hustle.

To the book clubs in Sacramento that have embraced me S.I.T.N.O.L., Literary Divaz, W.O.W., and also to Our Rightful Place, thank you so much for inviting me this past year to visit your clubs. I enjoyed myself. Hope to see you again soon.

Niyah Moore

Marcus Books in San Francisco, thank you for carrying Guilty Pleasures and I also look forward to the Fillmore Jazz Festival signing. That is going to be amazing. To Jason Frost over at Russo's Books, I look forward to also coming on down to Bakersfield. I enjoy networking with you.

To all my new readers, thank you guys for reading and keeping me busy. Without you all, I wouldn't have any feedback to feed off of.

To Cyrus Webb, thank you for having me on Conversations Live. Thank you to all the blog talk radio hosts that have featured me over the past year from Wine about Books to The1Essence Radio.

Blaze Reviews, thank you for keeping it oh so very real. That table talked helped. You rock!

To all my Tell Your Girl Blovel readers on wattpad.com, whew, you guys sure know how to keep that thing going. When will it ever stop? It's all good because I'm having so much fun with it.

Hey, now, I know I left some peeps out and I'm sure you'll tell me, but please please don't be mad at my heart. You can be mad at my mind 'cause y'all know I need some ginkgo biloba for this memory. Love y'all.

MAJOR JAZZ

Dedicated to Love,

The Fillmore,

Cameron, Ciera, and Londyn

PRAISE FOR MAJOR JAZZ

"...As a history buff and music lover, I loved it. From romance issues and the struggle of him wanting to be like his father in music, but not in love, internal struggle of wanting love, but not hurting that love 'cause when it comes down to it, love of music trumps love of the second her. To Black San Francisco and its history told correctly through false eyes." – David M. Good, Freelance Editor

"No one takes you on a satisfying journey the way Niyah Moore does. In Major Jazz, all of the senses of sight, smell, touch and taste are heightened and satiated through a recreation of a moment in time when life was simpler and music caressed the soul. With a descriptive and elaborate finesse that only a skillful writer can deliver, Niyah tempts the mind and the spirit to remember and reflect on love, culture, obsession, and all that *JAZZ*."
-Lorraine Elzia, Award Winning Author of *Mistress Memoirs* and *Ask Nicely and I Might*

A WORD FROM THE AUTHOR

When I was sixteen years old, I fell in love with the Harlem Renaissance. Langston Hughes, Zora Neale Hurston, and Dorothy West became my favorites. I deemed myself to be a renaissance girl because I played piano, clarinet, matured in my writing, and put my acting chops to the test on a theater stage. I was especially fascinated by the fact that Zora and I share the same birthday, January 7th. My year is 1981 and she was born in my year backwards, 1891. That was so dope to me. Not to say that I'm her reincarnated, but I definitely feel that our spirits are connected because of that reason.

As an adult, I've discovered that my passion for writing is something that comes more natural as it flows from this bottomless overflowing well that I call my soul. My passion for books about the Harlem Renaissance developed over the years. Once I found out we had a Harlem of the West right here in San Francisco, I was more than thrilled to find out everything I could. I felt inspired to write stories.

Fillmore Street in San Francisco was where the Jazz Era once thrived circa the 1940's and 50's, but today the neighborhood looks completely different from the way it looked then. I fell in love at first sight with the remodeled neighborhood. With jazz clubs like the Sheba Piano Lounge and Yoshi's, I felt this burning desire to call this place my new home. Fillmore Street has a very rich history and it reached out to me like a ghost wanting to be recognized for its mere presence. As evocative and scary as that seems, I wasn't afraid, but more excited than anything. As I walked along Fillmore Street, I stared at the markings on the sidewalk engraved with names and landmarks, noting the prolific Jazz Era; I found pieces of information that was more like a sip for my thirsty spirit.

At the library, I checked out a book called "Harlem of The West: The San Francisco Fillmore Jazz Era" by Elizabeth Pepin and Lewis Watts. Not only were the pictures inside of the book riveting, it was filled with interviews and testimonials of what it was like to live, dwell, and flourish around that time. Completely spellbound by what I read, my interest grew into an obsession. The love they had for jazz music and for the lifestyle of the Fillmore jumped out of those pages and became a part of me. I drew from what was said about Jimbo Edwards (owner of Bop City), Wesley Johnson, Sr. (owner of the Texas Playhouse and Flamingo Club), Leola King, (owner of the Blue Mirror), and Sugar Pie DeSanto (an African American and Filipino mixed singer born and raised in San Francisco).

Back then, the Victorian styled homes housed finely dressed men and women who owned their own businesses,

from cleaners to restaurants. They worked mornings during the week. At night, they enjoyed local musicians along with the likes of Charles Mingus, Jerome Richardson, Teddy Edwards, Duke Ellington, Billie Holiday, T-Bone Walker, John Coltrane, Dexter Gordon, and Pony Poindexter. Up and down Fillmore, clubs and restaurants lined up one after the other for blocks. On Friday nights, they went from club to party to bar until the wee hours of Monday morning.

But, then it all came to an end.

Jimbo Edwards said, "The time had run out. I was there fifteen years from 1950 to 1965 and the time was over. It was all over. The Blackhawk was closed. The Say When was closed. All the clubs was closed and the musicians didn't come to San Francisco. So then I was sitting with an empty club and nobody to draw from..."

The Housing Redevelopment Agency completely tore down all the buildings by the late sixties. Jack's Tavern and Bop City's buildings are still standing today. Bop City now houses Marcus Books and is located on Fillmore Street, around the corner from its original spot on Post. When I first walked into that place, I could imagine the energy that lived between the walls. Booming music was once alive and I tried to capture the magic. Jack's Tavern, now renamed the Boom Boom Room, used to be on Sutter, but is now on Fillmore Street.

MAJOR JAZZ

All of the other buildings are no longer around. How could something so magical vanish with very little trace of its existence? A small part of Fillmore Street has now been simply labeled the "The Jazz District", which is like a slap in the face to all who played there. It was more than just Jazz music. It was the Blues, R&B, and Bebop music; that's what it truly was.

Few are aware of Fillmore's more important musical "heyday" and that's why I felt the need to bring it back to life. Availing myself of my imagination, in the pages to follow, I have created what I feel represents my interpretation of this era because I wanted to write about falling in love with jazz and the neighborhood. The Fillmore Jazz Era may be gone, but it's certainly not forgotten. The love that once existed subsists and remains in the heart and soul of Fillmore forever. All I had to do was open my ears and listen to tell its amazing story.

-Niyah Moore

Conversational Piece
A poem

Waves in the midst of emotional inconspicuous opinions

Two encounters, two minds, amalgamated mutual forces to

form topics

She speculates his philosophy

He verbalizes

She pays heed

She expresses interest

He takes notes

…Nervous laughter eases the vibes

A dimly lit room, some wine, soft jazz, and gentle subtle

gestures of the hand

Elements that persists in the flow of passion

A path, inspired by one another or maybe it's the music…

Music of life, love, contentment, and sorrow…

He wonders when she closes her eyes if she can feel him

The saxophone, piano, and bass in the background

A musical melody he's referring to eloquently

Magic is in the making

Smiles so imposing

Sharing, finding what love once was,

meaningless, perhaps before

Love didn't feel like this, platonically speaking anyway

Uncomplicated as it feels, love has never felt this pleasant

Her heart skips to the same beat of his hi-hat drum

Her beauty is like no other he's ever known

His words carefully chosen uplifting her spirit

Candid waves leading to a shared dual passion unexplored,

an unfathomable conversation

Niyah Moore

JAZZ

Jazz, Dixieland, ragtime, rag, swing, jive, bop, bebop, big band music, jitterbug music, blues, rhythm and blues, boogie, boogie-woogie; hot jazz, le jazz hot, cool jazz, jazz rock, fusion music, syncopation, and improvisation.

The Aquino Sisters

We went out dressed to *kill*. You hear me? You couldn't tell us we weren't knockouts in our first-class clothes and nice hats. When we dressed, literally to the nines, baby, we strut our stuff! To Fillmore Street was where we were headed because the music called our names one by one: Lucille, Sallie, and Sade, in that order, from oldest to youngest, sisters. While we walked and laughed, never ending music poured into the streets out of the windows of our neighbors' houses. Music in the Fillmo' felt organic and it belonged to us and to the community.

That summer of '51, our neighborhood, the corner of Buchanan and Webster Street, was mixed and we didn't have any racial outbreaks of violence or madness of any kind. No, honey! The Jewish welcomed you into their delis and the Japanese rented to everyone in their hotels and rooming houses. They served you good in their restaurants. See, we came from a mixed background. My Filipino father and Black mother were hard-workin', great dressin', good dancin', and the most respectable people like the rest of the people in our neighborhood. Together, they raised us the best way they knew how, all while being the owners of Aquino's Cleaners on Fillmore Street.

As the baby sister, I was most stubborn and quick-tempered. I didn't take shit from anybody. As much as I enjoyed hot steamy nights with no good fast talkin' two timin' hustlers who razzed my berries from the pool halls, I still had my own mind, and didn't let anybody's dope or abusive ways stand in my way of a good time. No, sir, I didn't play around. I worked at our family's cleaners from early morning until closing, five days a week. When I was off work, I let my hair all the way down, you know, got real loose.

The oldest was Lucille and she had just graduated college. She was working at being a school teacher, but you couldn't let that preppy act fool you. She was one heck of a tough cookie, married to a jailbird, cursed like an angry drunk man when she felt the need, and was just as stubborn as a donkey.

Sallie, the middle child, was enrolled in beauty school and studied Cosmetology. From what everyone said, she was the prettiest out of the three of us. I begged to differ. The pretty one was me, but anyway, Sallie was madly in love with Major Ingram, a man who played the piano with everything he had inside of him. I didn't like to call her naïve, but sometimes I wondered if she really thought that man would ever be completely hers.

For sisters we were close, a year between each, best friends, and always broke beans together. What was mine was theirs and vice versa. What one didn't have, we came together to make sure she had. We walked down the street, a few blocks to the 'Mo, our playground. I remember it like it was yesterday. It was my twenty-first birthday. Men in long coats, satin ties, and Stacey Adams shoes with bleached white shoestrings saturated the streets. We were in a heaven of our own. Three ladies, the Aquino girls enjoyed our lives to the fullest whenever we possibly could. It was a night I'll never forget because it was not only the night I became legal to drink, it was also the night I met *him*.

I was wearing a dark flowered print dress and fancy pearl earrings that I borrowed from Lucille without asking. She saw them on my ears and rolled her eyes, but didn't say a word, though I knew she truly wanted to yank them off me.

We were almost near bootlegging Minnie's Can-Do, a petite nightclub. A Doo-Wop group was on the corner singing with perfect harmony. A lot of singing groups at that time showcased their talent up and down Fillmore Street, but that group in particular was real good. I gave them a wink and a smile as we passed them.

Lucille complained, "I'm starvin'. My stomach is talkin' as if I haven't fed it all day. I don't know why, but I'm craving some peach cobbler. What about y'all?"

"You sure you ain't pregnant?" I asked. "You've been cravin' peach cobbler all day."

Lucille sucked her teeth and replied nonchalantly, "I'm not pregnant."

"How you know? You've been to the doctor?"

"I don't need a doctor to tell me somethin' I already know!"

"Ever since your husband got out of jail, y'all sure have been sexin' a lot."

"It's called make-up sex. Mind your own damned business, Sade. If I'm pregnant, you'd be the first to know. Trust me, Daddy don't want any of us *whores* to get pregnant while still living under his roof. I'm too smart for that. Plus, Johnnie has to keep his ass out of jail long enough," Lucille asserted.

MAJOR JAZZ

I laughed at her. Johnnie didn't know how to keep his ass out of jail long enough. He was a dope dealing fool that spent the past five years going in and out and would probably spend the next five doing the same damned thing. There wasn't shit she could do about it.

"What's so funny?" Lucille asked while putting her hand down her blouse to scratch her double D's. "This powder got me itchy."

"I don't have to tell you how impossible it is to turn Johnnie into a square."

"I'm not trying to turn him into a square, Sade." Lucille then changed the sensitive subject, "What we gonna eat? I'm still starvin'."

Sallie offered a suggestion, "Ooooh, why don't we take our fine behinds on over to Bop City? They have a group deal, fried chicken in a basket for five dollars before midnight. You know how they run out of chicken all the time, so let's get goin'."

Besides showcasing the best sounds in the city, Jim sold fried chicken dinners. His fried chicken was something else and it sold out quick, but we knew the real reason why Sallie wanted to go to Bop City and it wasn't for Jim's bargain greasy fried chicken. She wanted to see *Major*. The chance she had of keeping his attention once we got there was slim, but she wasn't willing to give up without a grueling fight. She was more than determined to make that man hers and he didn't seem to be interested unless he wanted to get into her pants.

I hated to admit that Major Ingram was really gorgeous 'cause the way he shot Sallie down all the damned time was just plain embarrassing. Ole yella-skinned green-eyed talented motherfucker-- that's what he was to me.

Niyah Moore

We walked down three blocks, passing the Texas Playhouse, Town Club, Elsie's Breakfast Nook, and Havana Club along the way.

"Shit, Sallie, I'm tellin' you right now, we leavin' as soon as we eat. I don't want to stay all night while you wait for Major to look your way." Lucille threw her cigarette butt on the ground before we could go inside of Bop City.

Sallie tried to fight her smile while snatching my freshly lit cigarette before I could take the first puff. She took a long drag before handing it back to me. "I want some fried chicken and that's it. Ain't nobody thinkin' 'bout Major."

"Yeah, right... If Major was to fly off that stage and let you hop on his lap, I bet you wouldn't be trynna pretend you don't think about him," I chimed in, challenging her sly grin. "Plus, I want to go out dancin' tonight."

"We won't be here long, I promise. We can go dancin' afterwards."

Sallie was a lie. Whenever that man got on the piano, she would sit down like a lovesick stalker at the edge of the stage, underneath that piano, staring up at him while he played every single note. When he finished, if he wanted to be bothered with her, he would. If he didn't, he didn't.

I didn't have time to be fooling with nobody's musician, honey. Half of them were drunks or strung out on junk anyway. I wanted a regular man who had a regular job. I enjoyed the music, don't get me wrong, but dating someone on the music scene just wasn't for me.

You know the saying you can't go looking for love because love will find you? Well, that's the way it happened with me. I wasn't looking for love. Oh no!

Love found me at a time when I wasn't ready to be hit with cupid's 'ole foolish arrow.

We paid our dollar to Jim at the door once inside of Bop City. Everybody had to pay a dollar unless you were a musician. Musicians got in for free. Jim didn't play around with that rule either. If you looked like trouble, he didn't let you in, dollar or not. That was the main reason why there weren't any fights in Bop City.

It must've been sailor night because half of the men in there were dressed in their navy uniforms, laughing and drinking with pretty women in their company. There was one particular sailor who watched my every move from the moment we walked in the door. With disregard, I didn't acknowledge him because in order for me to give him a hello with my eyes, he was going to have to earn it. Lucille, Sallie, and I found the only vacant table in the house, but it wasn't cleaned yet. Evidence of the prior party's good time was all over-- a horrible mess.

"Can someone come clean this vicious table?" Lucille hollered towards the front with her face frowned up so bad you would think the table reeked of a foul odor.

"Ugh, don't make that face. You look just like Mother Dear," Sallie said.

Lucille fluttered her eyelashes and looked around the cramped room for someone to clean up. "Is this the only table available in the house?"

"Yep..." I popped my chewing gum and tried not to notice just how hard Mr. Chocolate Sailor was breaking his neck to take a glance at me.

He was surely checking me out. I tried to pay him no mind, well, up until he went and got the busboy himself to have the table cleaned. He stood in front of us like Superman when it was done.

"That was sweet of you," Sallie said. "Thank you."

"The pleasure is all mines."

When he smiled, his deep dimples jumped out at me. I couldn't help but become instantly attracted. There was something about that man's dimpled smile, uniform, and arrogant air that had my full attention. His skin looked just like rich milk chocolate, delicious enough to eat. His eyes were glued to my face as he asked, "Can I get you ladies something to drink?"

My sisters noticed right away that he couldn't keep his eyes off me. They smiled at one another; looking all silly like they had just discovered some great miraculous wonder.

"Jim don't sell no liquor up in here. We gotta go down to Long Bar for that," I answered quickly, pointing to the sign hanging up front. "That sign says no liquor sold or served on these premises."

"I have my own bottles at my table. Where does it say that that's against the rules?"

That wasn't against the rules. People always brought in their own liquor. I just wanted to be difficult. "Thanks, but no thanks."

"What the hell is wrong with you? We'll most certainly have a drink," Lucille declared. "Sade, sit your mean ass down and let this nice sailor, here, get us a drink."

I sat reluctantly, rolling my eyes at her.

"Sadeeeee," he sang. "That's a beautiful name."

"Why, thank you, suga." I winked at him.

"I'm Lucille and this is Sallie."

"It's definitely nice to meet you ladies. You all must be sisters. I can see the resemblance."

MAJOR JAZZ

"Thank you. It's nice to meet you, too," Lucille said.

Looking at him from head to toe, my eyes most certainly liked what they saw. Thoughts of getting my legs around his waist bombarded me. Yeah, I was hot in the pants. Hell, a girl like me relished in a good time.

With a straight face I asked, "What's your name, sailor?"

"Everybody calls me Hanes. My name is Jerome Hanes."

"How 'bout I call you J?" I licked my lips slowly, drinking him in from head to toe as if he were a Coca Cola.

He smiled wickedly, deep dimples in tow. "I like the sound of that. I'll be right back with your drinks."

Standing tall, he walked away with his shoulders back, head upright, and I could tell underneath those clothes he was well built like a running back of a football team. My corrupted mind was figuring out just how I wanted to make him my new play thing when he came back with three shot glasses of vodka.

I put my gum underneath the tabletop, a nasty habit my sisters hated, and gulped the shot. Lucille looked around for a waiter to order food, hungry heifer, as she sipped her liquor. Sallie knocked hers back and scanned the room for Major, pathetic clueless thing. Once she spotted him at the front door talking, her eyes never left him.

Jerome flashed me his smile and started to walk away from the table.

"I know you not gonna stroll off like that," I scowled as the good liquor burned my empty stomach. I wanted another shot. "It's my birthday."

"Well, birthday girl, you should join me at my booth. There's room for one more."

Niyah Moore

He didn't have to say it twice. I was ready to leave hungry hippo and love-struck duck right where they were. I sashayed over to his booth and he made space for me. I slid in next to him. Like electromagnets, we were drawn. A yearning inside of me intensified every time I stared into his penetrating eyes and at his dimpled grin. Couldn't help but flirt my ass off, I scooted close to his side. He didn't do anything else but put his arm around me.

"You're quite a beauty," he complimented while biting on his top lip.

His lips, succulent looking and plump, were begging for my lips to touch them.

"Where are you from?" I asked, noticing a hint of an accent in his voice. It wasn't southern or country sounding, just different.

"New Jersey. Where are you from?"

"I was born and raised in San Francisco, the Western Addition, mostly."

"I'm thinking about moving to the Western Addition. I like Fillmo'. The naval ship is stationed in Pleasanton. I have three weeks left before I'm discharged. I'm thinking about taking a job over at the Naval Air Station in Alameda."

"You got it made in the shade."

"I make a decent living, more than enough to survive."

"That's what life should be about, surviving." I took his bottle and helped myself to another shot.

"Have you eaten anything yet? You should have some of this food before you drink some more, don't you think?"

I reached over and grabbed a dinner roll from the middle of the table. "This will do the trick. I'll eat some chicken in a minute."

He watched me bite into that soft dinner roll. His eyes looked glazed as if he were imagining something else was in my mouth. I smiled because I could read his mind and it was just as dirty as mine. While he poured another shot for me, I placed my free hand right in his lap. Sure did. Bold, yes I know it, but like I said, I was already hot in the pants and he had me feeling a blaze. I felt him and he grew against the palm of my hand.

"What's goin' on in that pretty lil' head of yours?" He gently removed my hand from his lap and placed it in my own.

"Oh, you know what I'm thinkin' and seem to me you want it just as bad as I do. Only, you're fightin' it."

His eyes studied my earnest expression and I could tell he had never met a woman who was so forward, a woman who knew without a doubt what she wanted, and a woman who wasn't afraid to get it. He casually smiled, though I didn't recognize his gaze. Most men would've said, "Let's get out of here." Not him. Jerome Hanes played me cool like an ice box.

"There's plenty of time for that, sweetheart. For now, we're enjoying one another's company, listening to sounds, and drinking."

I looked across the table at another sailor with two women in his company, one on each side of him. Both women were laughing hysterically at whatever he was over there whispering about.

Major hopped on stage and said a few inaudible words to the bass, sax, and drummer. I think he was telling them what he wanted to play before he coolly sat at the piano. He played Dinah Washington's song, *Please Send Me Somebody to Love.* He took the mic from the stand on the side of the piano and said, "Show a hand for the lady. She's singing the blues tonight."

While the crowd applauded, I looked over at Sallie, who had gotten out of her seat to go to the front so she could be as close to that stage as possible. She wanted him to see her. *Oh Lord*, I thought. I hoped Major would give her the attention she was working so hard for.

A beautiful young girl made her way to the stage and stood next to Major and his piano. I had never seen her around or heard her sing before, but my interest wasn't on that stage. I wanted Mr. Sailor...

Turning back to him, I asked, "Where's your wife and kids? Back home in Jersey?"

"I don't have a family. I'm single."

I took another shot of vodka and tapped my hand lightly on the table. "Are you looking for a wife?"

"I'm not looking, but I do want a wife and kids as soon as I can. What about you, gorgeous? You married or have any children?"

I waved my hand at him. "Please, I'm allergic. I enjoy my life just fine the way it is."

"You're real pretty... *real pretty*. You all black?"

People always asked because of my slanted eyes and long hair, and because I just looked mixed up.

"My father is Filipino and my mother is Black."

"Oh yeah? Wow. I've never met anyone Black with a Filipino father. What's that like?"

"No different than anybody else I know. My father is a great man. You mind if I have a piece of that chicken now?"

He slid the basket over and handed me a plate. "Help yourself to *whatever* you like."

"J, I would help myself to *whatever* I like, except you keep playing real hard to get."

He laughed at me with those dimples so deep I could stick the tip of my finger in them. "I'm not playing hard to get. There's a time and place for everything, right?"

"True, but…"

"But what? You want to do dat thing right here?"

My eyebrows were raised. "We can do a lot of things… right here… right now…"

The people across from us heard me and I didn't give a flying rooster. I wasn't talking to them, so I continued to pretend as if they weren't there. Jerome, on the other hand, looked as if he had just been caught with his pants at his ankles. If his dark skin could've turned red with embarrassment he would've.

The girl on the stage was singing the hell outta that Dinah Washington song and that got me back to looking at the stage. When she was done, the whole room exploded. That's how it worked over at Bop City. If the crowd liked you, they cheered and if they didn't like you, they waved you off. She had a natural gift for singing and after that night she became Candy Cane Taylor, one of our neighborhood's finest singers.

"Right here? Right now?" Jerome asked as if he couldn't get that off his mind.

"That's right. You heard me." I took a bite of a fried chicken wing.

He whispered in my ear, "Be careful what you ask for. You may just get what you want."

"I *may*? Better yet, I *will*." I took his sailor cap off his head and placed it on my own.

He laughed as if I had just told some big tickle slapstick joke. "What shall I do with you, Sade?"

"I know plenty of things you can do *with* and *to* me… Why don't we get out of here so you can find out how to solve that problem you seem to be havin'?" I cuddled up closer to him and placed my face so close to his I could've nearly kissed him.

Niyah Moore

He didn't back down to my challenge. He actually wrapped his arm around me and grabbed my outer thigh while I kissed him. When I parted from him, his eyes became dreamy, and he uttered, "Let's go."

"Baby, now you cookin' with gas."

Sade

Heavy panting, serious groping, excessive fondling, and lust-filled kisses happened in the backseat of his Chevy. With all the dirty little flirting I did inside of Bop City, he couldn't resist me any longer. He would've been a fool to do so. Once he parked his ride on the curb near the park, we climbed in the back and started having real fun. I didn't care if I just met him and I didn't care if he didn't talk to me any more after the night was over. I was too wrapped up in the spur of the heated moment to let my emotions go spiraling out of control and have me thinking too much about something I couldn't control. My tongue explored the inside of his mouth while both of his hands were full of my plump behind. That sailor knew how to produce the loudest moans from me effortlessly. Flinging my shirt off and onto the floor, I smiled down at him.

For a moment, he caressed my back and inhaled my skin. "You smell so sweet like flowers or something."

"This new perfume I bought... I can't think of the name right now." I smothered his mouth with another deep tongue-kiss.

Jerome unfastened my bra and threw his opened mouth to my C-cupped breasts once they were exposed. I was trying to unbuckle his pants, but I was having a difficult time. Being cramped in the backseat of his car was messing up my flow. He helped me by undoing his belt and easing his pants below his knees.

I hiked up my skirt, pushed my panties to the side, and maneuvered on top of his thickness. When I first felt him inside of me, I let out the most sensual noise I had ever made. He did all the work, thrusting his hips up against me. He was a fantastic lover, the best lover I had ever encountered. I could tell, even in the backseat of that car that I wasn't going to just want to have a one-night stand with him.

"Sweet Jesus..." I moaned up to the heavens.

"I told you to be careful what you ask for."

"Yeah..." I gasped, "Ohhhhh...."

We both were breathing real hard and couldn't catch our excited breaths because we were so stimulated and ready to get to Orgasmic City in a hurry. It didn't take us long before we both erupted and scorched the seats as if we were volcanic hot lava.

I lay there on top of him and we listened to one another take turns breathing. All of the windows were foggy and we couldn't see anything out of them. Jazz was still playing from the radio. I hadn't noticed it was on until we were resting in one another's arms. He moved away the messy bangs that were plastered to my forehead.

"I love jazz music," he said, playing in my hair. "That's why I like goin' to Bop City. One of my shipmates took me when he started taking liberty over here. I wish I had an ear to play, but I'm tune deaf." He chuckled. "What about you? What kind of music do you like?"

"I enjoy all types, really, but blues is my favorite. I love Muddy Waters and I like goin' to Bop City, too. Sometimes, I've been able to run into a few famous people while there."

Niyah Moore

"Yeah, Pony Poindexter was down there a few weeks ago, and man, I was in awe. I've witnessed some heavy jam sessions."

"Me too…" I kissed his chin. "How old are you?"

"I just turned twenty-five in May. How old are you?"

"I just turned twenty one today."

He smiled. "That's right. Are you enjoying your birthday?"

"I am now…"

His face turned real serious as he said, "I'm fixing to check into a hotel and I want you to spend the night with me. I don't have to be on base 'til tomorrow morning around eleven…"

"It sounds like someone isn't ready to leave me just yet."

"Not yet… I'm enjoying the birthday girl's company. Is that fine by you?"

"That's fine by me. You ready?"

We put our clothes back on and he drove to the Booker T. Washington Hotel where he booked a room on the sixth floor-- the very top of the building. It was fancy. I was impressed, but I didn't let on that I was impressed.

He pressed my body up against the wall, slid his hands between my legs, and pulled my panties off. "There's something 'bout you that has me hooked already. This, right between your legs, is so good."

Against his lips, I said, "You can have it all, baby."

"Any time I want?"

"Any time you want it."

"I want it to belong to me."

"It's yours."

MAJOR JAZZ

He lifted me up and I wrapped my legs around his waist. As my back rested up against the wall, he had managed to unbuckle his pants and place himself inside of me. I moaned. It was like he couldn't get enough of me as I couldn't get enough of him, truth be told. There was no pulling us apart because we were inseparable. I made up my mind that any time he wanted to take liberty, we were going to meet at Bop City, leave in his car, and stay all night in a room at the Booker T.

Sade

Y ou can't keep your damned legs closed to save your life!" Lucille pointed her finger in my face.

Lucille wanted to meet up to do some shopping at GallenKamp's two mornings later. We finally had the chance to talk about it. I couldn't believe she was trying to act like she wouldn't have done the same thing if she were me.

I threw my head back and let out a good laugh. "Please, Lu Lu... You see how fine he is."

"I don't care if he's the finest thing walking on God's green earth... Neckin' in the car? You need to slow your hot ass down."

"Maybe he'll be the man to slow me down."

"Ha! You've known him all for what, a few nights, and you talking crazy like this? Chile, get out of here." She waved her chubby hand in the air before picking up a cute teal blouse off the rack.

"...He's not like anyone I've ever met before."

"How many times have I heard that spell?"

I rolled my eyes at her before snatching the same blouse she tossed back on the rack to take a look at it. "This time feels so real. He has a career goin' for himself."

"Military men can't be trusted, bottom line. All they do is make you they wife, knock you up, and get the next tramp pregnant right up under your nose."

"Oh, like your precious Johnnie?"

Her slanted eyes nearly bulged out of her head. "We weren't married yet when he got Vera pregnant and she miscarried."

"And that makes it okay?" I mumbled under my breath.

She heard me, rolled her eyes, and walked briskly between the aisles as she looked for something else to catch her eye. I put the blouse back since it wasn't the right size. Lucille wore two sizes larger.

"Mother Dear wants you to help her clean the china by noon," I called after her.

"You're such a liar. She told you to do it. I heard her this morning!"

"Why does she want me to do it?"

"Because it's your turn and Daddy's sisters will be here from the Philippines. She wants to impress them."

"Nothing Mother Dear ever does is good enough for them. In their eyes, she's still just a Negro woman."

Lucille spun around and looked at me with evil in her eyes. "Why do you always talk like that about our family?"

"Shit, it's true. Mother Dear's skin is nowhere near as dark as theirs, yet she's still too black for them."

"I hate it when you talk like that."

"Well then don't listen 'cause I'm gonna say what I feel."

Lucille sighed heavily before continuing her search inside of the large department store. "Where's Sallie? She was supposed to meet us here."

"She said somethin' 'bout helping Major with somethin'. She should be here any minute."

"What she helping Major for? I swear he uses her up every time she let him."

"That, my dear sister, is none of our business."

Niyah Moore

She grunted and placed her hand on her hip as she took a hard look at some dresses. "Why do they always make these things to fit tiny women? What does a full-figured woman like me have to choose from?"

"Clearly, not much… Why don't you just try to lose a few pounds, Lu Lu?"

"Why don't you just shut your big ass mouth about it?"

"I'm not the one always opening up my god-damned mouth 'bout my weight. You should really do somethin' 'bout it."

"Go to hell, Sade."

"Humph," I huffed.

"I know you feel chewed."

"Hey, I'll gladly go to hell as long as I can take a fine ass man like J with me. I hold my dress up to my knees, and I give my poontang to who I please."

"You're such a slut."

She didn't want to talk about how loose she got every time her husband went to jail.

"Let's not talk, dear sister. I'm not nearly as slutty as you are."

She clenched her teeth, narrowed her eyes at me, and made a slashing gesture at my behind. "How much split you want back here?"

"Good God, I can hear you two whores all the way down the aisle. The mouths on you two are just terrible," Sallie said as she walked up behind us.

Lucille interrogated roughly, "Why in the hell do you have to go breakin' your back for Major every time he asks you to?"

Sallie rolled her eyes and placed her weight on her right leg. "Major wants me to help him with Candy Cane Taylor. You know the one that was singing that

Dinah Washington song the other night? That girl has one hell of a voice on her and she's so pretty."

"Do you think he's screwin' her?" I scowled with a deep frown.

"No, she's just a child and still in high school."

"What the hell does that mean? Lu Lu met Johnnie when she was in high school and he was a grown man. He was always screwin' her."

"Why do you always have to bring Johnnie into everything?" Lucille fussed at me.

"I don't."

"Yes, you do. Plus, I thought we were talking about Major and him screwin' that girl."

Sallie interjected, "Major isn't screwin' her. He only has eyes for me."

Lucille and I looked at one another and laughed so hard. She was blind, honey. Major only had one thing on his mind most of the time-- music business. Pussy and liquor was the second and third.

Sallie looked hurt that we were laughing like hyenas, but we didn't care. Why sugar-coat the truth? She knew Major Ingram spread himself around. The whole neighborhood knew it.

"What you shopping for now, Lu?" Sallie hissed. "Don't you have enough party clothes to last you for a good while?"

"No... Nothing fits anymore and Johnnie is taking me out later."

"All he gonna do is take your clothes off before you can make it out of the door," I joked.

Lucille flashed me her usual evil glare as she emphasized, "I really need my sisters to help me find something to wear. Is that too much to ask for? Plus, everything I own seems to be fitting too tight."

"You're pregnant!" I declared.

Niyah Moore

"Stop with the pregnancy talk. You might jinx me…. Ooooh, look at this dress. Now this is nice."

Sallie nodded at the crème-colored chiffon cocktail dress. "Go try it on and make sure those big jugs fit in it."

Lucille strolled off toward the dressing room while we giggled at her. She was putting on more weight by the day, seemed like, and with all the eating she had been doing it wasn't a surprise.

I looked at Sallie and she was staring off into space with a cheesy grin. "What's got you so gleeful?"

"Major and I have a date tonight. I'm real jazzed 'bout it."

"He finally asked you out?"

"Yes, this morning."

"You spent the night with him?" I asked, realizing Sallie hadn't come home.

She giggled. "Yes."

"So, he finally got you. What took the bastard so long to ask you out?"

"You know he's been busy composing tunes, but he found some time for me. I told you if I was patient he would come around."

"You look happy. You know what you gonna wear?"

"I already know what I'm wearing. Hey, you should come with us and bring your new friend."

"Who?"

"Mr. Sailor…"

"J won't be on liberty until the weekend."

"Well, Major is throwing a house bash this weekend. See if he wants to go."

"I'll run it by him."

"Swell…How was he the other night, by the way?"

MAJOR JAZZ

I shrugged because I didn't want to get the same reaction I got from Lucille. "I shot him lightly and he died politely."

Sallie studied me and laughed, but before she could give her opinion, Lucille came out of the dressing room. The dress was extremely flattering and gorgeous on her curvaceous body.

"Hot thaaaang." I whistled with my two fingers.

She turned crimson as she tried to conceal her smile. "I'm gonna buy it. What you think, Sallie?"

"I love it. Now hurry the hell up. I want to grab some lunch. Where y'all want to go?"

I replied with my voice dragging, "I have to go help Mother Dear clean the china."

"What about you, Lu?" Sallie asked.

"I'll have lunch with you. What you feel like eating?"

"Fried chicken..."

"Hell no!" Lucille shouted.

I waved at them and laughed. "Bye heifers. I'll see y'all later before Mother Dear throw a fit."

Sade

I s that you, Sade?" Mother Dear called from
the kitchen.
"Yeah, it's me." I closed the front door
behind me, put my coat on the rack, and tossed my keys
in the glass bowl where all the keys went.

The smell of good food filled my nostrils. I
knew that smell all too well. Ground pork, onions,
cabbage, minced carrots, black pepper, crushed garlic,
green onions, and soy sauce filled my nose. The filling
for Lumpia, our traditional Filipino dish, was cooking
on the stove. That meant one thing and one thing only.
Our aunts, Beatrice and Gilda, had already arrived.

Their loud chatter soon greeted me before I
could reach the kitchen.

"Get in here, Sadeeeeeee," Beatrice sang.

"Don't yell at her. Wait 'til she gets in here to
talk," Gilda snapped.

I was happy to see my aunts, but I hated to see
the way Mother Dear had her head lowered and what
looked like welled up tears behind her eyes as she
washed the china. Whatever my two aunts were
discussing with my mother before I got there was the
cause. I hated the way they complained to her about
everything they felt like griping about.

Aunt Bea was preparing to wrap Lumpia and
Aunt Gilda was prepping for her famous Chicken
Adobo. Immediately, they started speaking Tagalog to
one another with sly smiles on their faces. I understood
just a little bit and they were talking badly about me.

They knew I was fully aware, but that didn't stop them from gossiping. No surprise.

I hugged them anyway. "Good to see you Auntie Bea and Auntie Gilda."

Aunt Bea smiled. "You look beautiful. Come, help me wrap."

"Where your sisters?" Aunt Gilda questioned.

I washed my hands in the sink next to Mother Dear. She didn't smile at me, matter of fact, her eyes stayed on the dishes she was cleaning. I never understood my mother's silence when it came to my father's sisters. Mother Dear's four sisters were strong and boisterous women, the opposite of her, and they knew how to stand their ground. I felt like swift kicking her to put it into her.

"Lucille and Sallie went to have lunch."

Aunt Bea made a "tsk" sound when she clicked her tongue. "Why they eating elsewhere? We make all this food."

"Did they know we are here?" Aunt Gilda asked with a deep scowl.

"No... But they knew you would be here some time today." I dried off my hands.

"You can start out of this bowl... Cool down enough to handle," Aunt Bea smiled.

As soon as I placed the filling in a wrap, Aunt Gilda complained, "Don't overstuff. You put too much."

I flashed a look of irritation to let her know not to start with me. She gave me the same look, which was identical. Everyone always said I looked just like her, except she was a shade darker.

"Lillian, what time does Melcher get off work?" Aunt Bea interrogated.

Mother Dear remained silent as if she wasn't asked a single question.

I replied, "Father usually comes home after seven. He likes to close the cleaners himself."

"Ah, he works too hard. That's good," Aunt Gilda patted my shoulder. "Lillian, would you mind handing me that garlic?"

Mother Dear handed her the clove of garlic and then walked to the bathroom down the hall.

"What's the matter with Mother Dear?" I asked them.

I wanted to hear their answers because I knew they were the ones responsible for her solemn mood.

"Lily was that way when we got here," Aunt Bea replied with a shrug.

"Maybe she's tired. I think she should take a rest," Aunt Gilda added.

Silence fell upon the kitchen. The only sounds were Aunt Gilda chopping garlic and Aunt Bea stirring inside that sizzling skillet. I didn't believe them for one moment. The two of them always bullied Mother Dear without thinking they were bullying her. I wished she would just stand up for herself once.

The front door opened. Sallie and Lucille came in arguing.

"Why does it have to be your way or no way at all?" Lucille yelled.

Sallie fired back, "I want to eat fried chicken."

"I have the chicken blues fuckin' 'round with you."

"You didn't say what you wanted to eat. We were right by Bop City and chicken seemed to be the easiest thing to grab."

"Why must we always go to Bop City? There are over a dozen restaurants 'round here. Why can't you just say you want to see Major? Shit, I have a taste for steak right now."

"I don't even like steak and I don't want to see Major," Sallie replied.

"Then why in the hell do we have to eat chicken at Bop City all of the damned time?"

"Hey, your aunts are here," Aunt Bea shouted over them.

Lucille and Sallie made their way into the kitchen quickly.

"It smells so good. I'm starving," Lucille said while grabbing a spoon and taking a heaping amount of Lumpia filling into her mouth.

"Sweet hog," Aunt Gilda frowned and then pinched Lucille's stomach before taking the spoon from her. "I hear your husband is out of jail, so you must be pregnant."

"Heavens, no!" Lucille gently moved out of Aunt Gilda's reach.

My Aunts were slim and would never allow themselves to gain a pound, even after having their children. They frowned upon gaining too much weight for any reason.

"Sallie, you're getting too dark," Aunt Bea griped.

"I've been tanning out at the beach for the last few days. I'm enjoying the sun while I can this summer."

I couldn't believe Aunt Bea had the nerve to say anything about getting dark. She was still darker than Sallie's new summer tan. My father's family was naturally darker than my mother's family, who were lighter-skinned African Americans from a Mulatto background.

"Try not to get too *tanned…*"

Niyah Moore

"Auntie Bea," Sallie forced a smile. "I will try my best not to."

"Where's Mother Dear? I want to show her my new dress before Johnnie gets home," Lucille said.

"She's in the bathroom," Aunt Gilda replied. "Go check on her. She's been in there for a little while."

Lucille went down the hall while Sallie washed her hands. "I'll finish washing these dishes for Mother Dear."

The week couldn't go by fast enough and my aunts' visit always made the air too tight around the house. Mother Dear hardly spoke a word and Father stayed at work longer hours to avoid them. Lucille wanted to spend time with Johnnie when she got done at the school house, but that was like trying to milk a duck, and when Sallie got out of school, she went off doing whatever Major wanted her to do. That left me to deal with the evil witches. Lucky me.

Sade

Friday night came and I couldn't wait to meet my sailor for a blast. My aunts' constant nagging left me sour, but he quickly turned my mood around. When he picked me up from home, he came in casual wear, jeans and a sweater, instead of his Navy uniform. He gave me a bouquet of red roses before we went over to Major's apartment for his bash.

It was my first time at Major's apartment. His place was so tiny and filled with cigarette smoke. I wasn't sure how all those people fit inside, but we were in there, snug as a rug. Major played some nice dance records while we made ourselves cozy in the corner on a sofa. Couples danced, people had some drinks, and laughter was all around us.

While I stared into Jerome's eyes, I wondered if he got better looking since the last time I saw him because it seemed that way. Maybe my mind altered his appearance because I couldn't remember him being so handsome. The smile I wore on my face let him know I was more than happy to see him again.

He whispered in my ear, "I've been thinking about you all week… couldn't wait to see you this weekend."

I responded by flicking my tongue against his lips. He gave me the deepest kiss in return.

"Your lips set me on fire," he said.

"Do they?"

"Yeah, kiss me again."

Lost in the heat of it all, I indulged in his kiss for another minute.

Sallie waved from across the room at us. I waved back. "There goes my sister, Sallie."

Jerome smiled and waved. "Where's your other sister?"

"Lucille and her husband, Johnnie, should be here soon."

Major walked up to Sallie with a glass of clear liquor in his hand and placed a small kiss on her forehead before he mingled with other guests.

"Is Major her boyfriend?"

"No, he strings her along and I don't think he likes her as much as she likes him."

"I can see him being that way... Do you want anything to drink?"

I nodded with a smile. "Does he have any more vodka?"

"I can go check."

"There, in the kitchen, I believe Major has some. See if he got some juice, too."

"I'll be right back." He gently grazed the side of my face with the back of his hand before getting up.

He had a way with sending magnificent chills down my spine, but I shook them off and a smile took over. Sallie made her way through the thick room and sat in Jerome's spot.

"I see the sailor knows how to keep a smile on your face," she said.

"He sure does. Hey, Major's pad sure is full tonight."

"Major's parties are always full."

"I'm so glad you two made up after that horrible dinner date. Is he your man yet?"

Sallie told me how he got mad at her when he felt like she insulted his music and he left her sitting in the restaurant on their very first date. Major's mood swings were unpredictable and if I was Sallie, I would've left his dumb ass alone.

"No…"

I noticed the saddened look in her eyes as she stared across the room. Major was flirting with a woman named Ginger as if Sallie wasn't there. I didn't want to tell her that I saw him around town with Ginger every now and then because I knew it would crush her. Rumor had it that they were an item at one time. It was also rumored she delivered their baby, stillborn. I didn't know if they were still screwing around or not, but by the looks of things, they might've been.

"Major will always be Major." She shrugged as if it were no big deal.

"How much do you really know about Major Ingram and Ginger Robinson?"

Sallie shrugged again. "I don't care, really."

"Yes, you do. Why do you think your eyes are welling up with tears?"

She fought those tears hard. When she blinked, a few managed to escape, but she wiped them away quickly and adjusted her sadness with a big deep breath. "Major is a man and women are constantly throwing themselves at him. Major will never be my man."

"But, you want him to be."

"Of course I do, Sade, but I have to face it. Major will never be all mine. He's all about his *music*…"

"You're in love with him, aren't you?"

"What does love have to do with anything?"

"Everything… Love is the reason why you cry. I hate to see you cry. Why don't you start seeing someone else?"

MAJOR JAZZ

"Like who?"

"I don't know. Shit, anybody else."

Major kept right on flirting away, smiling in Ginger's face as she laughed at almost everything he said with her hand on his. If I hadn't known any better I would say that Sallie's slanted eyes were filled with hatred for Ginger Robinson.

Jerome was back with a cup of gin. "Sade, he doesn't have any more juice. Sallie, would you like something to drink?"

"I've had enough to drink for the night. Thank you."

Jerome flashed us his dimpled grin. "You're welcome."

The song, *Sixty Minute Man*, by The Dominoes played. The bragging of sexual prowess on the record drove me wild. It was number one on the R&B charts at that time and number seventeen on the pop singles charts. Anyone who wasn't dancing started dancing. My favorite part was the chorus:

They'll be fifteen minutes of kissin'
Then you'll holler "Please don't stop"
(Don't stop)
They'll be fifteen minutes of teasin'
Fifteen minutes of squeezin'
And fifteen minutes of blowin' my top.

"Come on J, dance with me," I said getting up from the sofa.

I did the boogie-woogie along side of him before he took hold of my waist and led me to roll my hips in front of him. There would be no swing dancing with him. He wanted to grind and was light on his feet. He sure could cut a rug. His hands traveled along my hips as we danced to that rock and roll record as if no one else was in that room but us.

Niyah Moore

***

It wasn't long before we left and headed over to the Booker T. Hotel to finish what we started in Major's living room. I let his tongue explore me like no other. As he slid between my thighs, he licked me until I couldn't endure any more. Felt like I was mountaineering the walls and I'm sure everybody on that floor heard me howling. That was just the warm up, I discovered. When he gave me his sex, I felt the purest form of ecstasy one could feel. He could make love for what seemed like forever.

"Baby, I think that record, *Sixty Minute Man*, was written 'bout you..." I exasperated.

He covered my mouth with his kisses to shush me. He didn't want to hear any more talk, only moans of bliss. To see me breathless while in our wild love making ignited a sexual beast inside of him. My eyes rolled in the back of my head as he discovered the softest spot inside of me that drove me to the brink of insanity.

He rested in my arms as soon as we were finished. We were both too worn out to do anything else. With his sugary kisses placed on the top of my breasts, I giggled in delight. I loved his affection.

"I could spend every single night in your arms," he said, sincerely.

"You say that like you mean it."

"I mean what I say, woman... Wouldn't you like to spend every single night in my arms?"

"I don't know..."

He lifted his head a little, enough to see my eyes. For a brief moment, I could see the jumbled up confusion. His words spilled out of him as if he couldn't help it, "I want you to be my wife."

"Quit foolin' around." I laughed at how silly that seemed since we just met a week previously.

"I don't play around with anything so heavy. I want to marry you."

"I think people should only get married when they're in love and there's no possible way you could be in love with me, Jerome Hanes."

"I want to fall in love with you one day, Sade. Will you allow for that to happen?"

"I'm here, aren't I? I'm open to one day loving you with everything I have, just not right now."

He rested against my chest and squeezed me as if he didn't want to let go of me. "Fine, we shall do this your way, but just know that I always get my way eventually."

I hummed while caressing the top of his head. "You're some kind of special."

"Am I? How special am I to you?"

I glided my tongue over his lips before kissing him with every bit of passion I owned.

His smile broadened. "You blow my mind... Say, I've been thinking. I'll be out of the military in a few weeks and working at the Alameda base. I'm looking to buy this house and all I'm missing is a wife."

He was back to that wife talk and though it truly terrified me, I played him cool, by answering the best way I could, "You want to be the one to tame the wild beast inside of me?"

"Don't you want to be tamed?"

"God, no! I'm too wild to be somebody's wife."

"You wouldn't just be somebody's wife. You would be my wife."

"You want me to be a sailor's wife? Sailors can't be trusted-- too much temptation while at sea."

Niyah Moore

"Let me put it to you this way, I've been on sea, sowed my wild oats, and I'm going inactive. I'll have a job on base until I retire and I'll be able to be at home with you and the babies."

"What babies? Whew, now you're bashing my ears."

"Aw, come on. You don't dream of having babies?"

With a serious face I replied, "I do not dream of having babies."

"Not even for me?"

As I stared at him with those deep dimples, I couldn't help but actually consider his dream. He was that fine to me. Fine enough to make me change my mind about settling down and starting a family. How bad could it be to spend the rest of the night with a man I felt fireworks for?

Using my stirred up passion, I brought the side of his face up to my lips. With that kiss, I gave him the answer he wanted to hear. He wrapped his arms around me tightly and rolled over so I could wind up on top of him.

"I'm your man now, baby."

"Whatever you want is what you get, huh? Is there any other way with you?"

His smile, ever so sexy, he replied, "There may be a few loopholes, but I truly have to have it my way or no way at all."

"You're leaving me with no other choice?"

"You got it now, baby doll."

He squeezed me tightly in his strong arms and those muscles made me feel truly safe and secure. Every time I was in his arms, the world seemed to be a perfect place.

MAJOR JAZZ

Lucille

I wasn't the one to take nobody's mess, but when it came to my husband, I had a hard time showing him just how fed up I was getting. I needed to, according to what my sisters kept telling me, but this was my life and I was going to live it the way I pleased. He truly should've had another thing coming if he thought I was going to keep letting him come home in the wee hours of the morning, stumbling drunk, and smelling like another woman. Putting him out seemed only right, but I had yet to do it. Mother Dear guessed I just wasn't good and tired yet.

I was sitting in my bed with the lights on, waiting for his sorry self to come home. We missed Major's party because of him. Instead of going to the party alone, I stayed home with my nerves all in a wreck, wondering where in the hell he could be. Just when I thought he might've landed his tail back in jail, I heard the front door slowly creak open at two o'clock in the morning. I could tell he was trying to come in as quietly as possible by the sound. Soon after, his heavy boots thudded down the hallway. He was making too much noise and the last thing I wanted was for my parents to wake up. They already warned me that if he kept coming in late we would have to move, and rent was too expensive for me to manage on my own.

Johnnie did what he wanted. He came in late every night for as long as we lived there, a rule he just couldn't seem to abide by.

I hopped out of bed onto my bare feet, wrapped my bathrobe around me tighter, flung open the bedroom door, and met him in the hallway before anyone else could. With both hands on my hips, I truly wanted to scream at him, but I spoke slightly above a loud whisper instead. "Do you know what time it is? Where you been, Johnnie?"

He looked pathetic as he mumbled something I couldn't make out underneath his breath, stumbling down the long narrow hall to our bedroom. Catching a whiff of the putrid stench of the liquor he had been drinking all night, I held my nose and mouth to stop me from gagging.

"Johnnie… you need to take your stinky behind in there and take a bath before you get in the bed with me."

He lost his balance and fell on his back right before he could walk into the room. He groaned loudly, "Lu, I'm drunk… as a skunk! Help me…"

"I know it... Shhhh, you're going to wake up the whole house."

The hall light flickered on. "I'm already awake." Mother Dear's cold eyes pierced through me while I was trying to help Johnnie up. "Now, hurry up and get him out this hallway… Please… don't wake anyone else."

Far from being a little man, Johnnie weighed two hundred and forty-five pounds and stood over six feet tall. How in the hell was I supposed to get him up all by myself and quietly? The more I struggled to get him on his feet, the more noise he seemed to make. Because of his drunken stupor, it seemed almost impossible.

"Mother Dear, I can't get him up."

She took Johnnie up under his arms and nodded her head for me to grab his feet. In a whisper she said, "If your father wakes up…. he's not going to be too happy about his sleep being disturbed. Lord, forbid your wicked aunts if they wake up. We will never be able to stop them from bad talking."

With Mother Dear's help, we were able to get Johnnie in the bed. As I tussled with his heavy boots to get them off, she stared at me. "How much longer are you going to endure this, Lucille?"

Taking in a little air, I held my head up high and tucked in my bottom lip. I couldn't help that I loved the damned fool. "He's my husband, so let me deal with him. Good night, Mother Dear."

Mother Dear didn't say another word while she closed the bedroom door gently, turned off the hall light, listened to the house to see if anyone else had been awakened, and then returned to her own bedroom to find that Father hadn't been disturbed by Johnnie's racket. Thank heavens.

I took off Johnnie's slacks next and griped with a scowl, "Why are you so stupid, jackass?"

A large wad of money and small individual bags of what looked like drugs dropped out of his pocket onto the floor. I could feel my chest tighten up as it rose and then fell heavily. He promised not to hustle or deal heroin on the streets anymore. All of my yelling, screaming, and threatening to leave him was all a waste of time. He told me a big fat lie. The fact that he was never going to be nothing but a hoodlum rocked my core so that it really pained me, starting from the tip of my toes to the top of my crown.

Abrupt tears flowed down my face as I hurried and stuffed the mess back into his pockets before he could realize my discovery. His snores confirmed that he was asleep just that fast and he had no idea about what I found. I felt like tossing a boiling pot of water on top of him. The thought that I could wake him up from his inebriated slumber and burn the stench he reeked of from his golden brown skin delighted me.

Lying beside him, I fumed and felt small flutters inside of my tummy. That wasn't the first time I felt those weird flutters. I tried so hard to ignore what was going on inside of my uterus, but it seemed like everyone else knew before I could own it. I was very much pregnant and was too afraid to tell anyone. Seemed as if I didn't have to tell anyone, they all could see it. Two doctors confirmed it. The bottom line was that I didn't want Johnnie to leave or go back to jail, so I wasn't going to tell him.

With my hand holding onto the fluttering going on, I closed my eyes and prayed for the baby to never be fatherless. Though his father was surely an idiot, in just a few short months, I wasn't going to be able to hide it anymore.

Johnnie wrapped his arms roughly around me. He was too heavy, sweaty, and stinky to be all over me that way, so I squirmed to try to get away, but he was too strong.

"Johnnie…"

I had to find some sort of comfort under his heavy arm, but that was impossible.

"Nooo," he whined.

"Don't move, baby…"

"Johnnie, I can't breathe."

More snores from him…

As the pain in my gut mounted to heighten my silly sadness, the only thing I could do was cry myself to sleep.

Sallie

What do I have to do to get you to love me, huh?" I asked Major the one question that seemed, to me, like a simple question.

Love was supposed to be easy. I knew without a shadow of doubt that Major Ingram was the only man I loved. When I was intimate with him, I gave him all of me and though his mouth told me he cared for me just as much, his arduous ways were bothersome. I felt that if I continued to love him intensely that in time he would do the same, but I was starting to give up. How long would I have to wait for him to be ready?

With both of my hands holding his handsome face, I stared into those picturesque hazel eyes and waited for his response. We were alone, for the moment, in his apartment. It would only be a few minutes before the band would show up to start rehearsing for the gig he had with Candy Cane Taylor.

"What you talking about, woman? I love you."

What a typical Major response, I thought to myself. "Humph, I can hardly tell… I want you to love *only* me… Is that too much to ask for?"

His concentrated eyes seemed bottomless, yet full of passion as he continued to stare through me. He caused all the blood to rush through me and my heart started pounding. Biting on his lower lip, he then inched in to plant a brief moist kiss on my lips. Right after his sweet kiss, he uttered, "Nothing is too much to ask for… But you know I can't love you the way you want me to right now… I just need a little more time."

I was growing tired of his games. My heart wasn't anything to be played with and my feelings were real. I wasn't sure if he realized that. His nonchalant attitude pinched a nerve that had me ready to curse him out. With both hands on my hips, I questioned, "A little more time for what, Major? Are you still seeing Ginger?"

He sighed, but his facial expression remained stern. "Ginger is a good friend of mine. You know that."

Then, he sat at the piano to play.

I wouldn't let up as I leaned across the top of his baby grand to get his attention. "Are you still mad about what happened at the Champagne Supper Club between me and Ginger?"

On our first date, he took me to the Champagne Supper Club and Ginger was there. We got into it over him and he didn't like that one bit.

He shook his head, kissed me on the cheek, and gently got me to move out of his way by nudging my shoulder.

I know I probably sounded silly pleading for his affection, but I did so anyway. "I need you to tell me how you feel about me."

The stern look on his face told me to stop sounding so pitiful. Once I backed up some, he played classical and that stopped me from wanting to start a fight with him. In the opening bars, he played long, loud descending runs before going extremely fast with mainly his left hand, and his build up to the main theme became recognizable.

I gasped. "You know Chopin?"

"Revolutionary Etude is one of my favorite pieces. If you truly knew how angry Chopin was when he wrote this…"

"You play it beautifully."

The way his fingers of his left hand and head moved to the rapid pace of the song was passionate, much like the way he made love. He had mastered the piece. For the first time, I noticed that Major was left handed. I didn't know why I hadn't noticed it before.

"Chopin poured his emotions into many pieces composed in 1831. This piece stands out as one of the most notable examples."

Astounding how he could talk and not mess up one note of the complicated tune for three minutes. I sat on a chair and listened. His interpretation was magical. The way he shaped the passages brought a fresh feel to the masterpiece. He ended the piece with a dark and quiet preparation of the final sweep with both of his hands descending to a C major chord. Bravo.

I clapped with a smile on my face. "That was so good. You are amazing. Are you left handed?"

He laughed. "Yes… You didn't know that?"

"I just noticed."

"You don't love me then." He chuckled.

I laughed at him. "I do love you. It's just that you use both hands equally, but that piece requires mostly left hand work…"

"There are right handed people that can nail that piece just as well."

"Why'd you choose to play that one?"

"I played that piece because you want to know how I feel about you… Take what you want from it."

I thought of the great composition. It was full of energy, anger, and captured the essence of the Revolution. Complex, like his love for me, I could feel his heart through it and even though it confused me further, it pacified me for the time being. He decided to play it again for me, just in case I missed his hidden message behind the music. I heard his heart louder than I had the first time. He was at war, stuck between loving two women and loving his music. He was having a full on battle of his own feelings. Before my teary eyes could let a tear drop, there was a knock at his front door. The band had arrived.

Sade

Jerome was officially honorably discharged and working on base in Alameda. He bought a house in Lake Merritt before summer could officially be over. We talked of marriage some more, but I wasn't quite ready. I was still partying and living my life. One night, he was working on base pretty late and I was out with Sallie, drinking at the Texas Playhouse.

I sat at the infamous bar with $3,500 in silver dollars embedded into the top of it and murals of musicians in silver leaves all around it. I was flirting with a man I had slept with once before. He went by the name of Shooter because he had shot a few people in the past and got away with it. I didn't care about none of that. All I cared about was that drinks kept flowing and Wes kept spinning those hit dance records from his jukebox.

The place was filled to the brim. We were lucky to even get in through the long line outside. Ladies were always free and the men weren't allowed in without a jacket and tie. Wes liked to keep the place upscale. I was so intoxicated that I had to remain on the stool to hold me steady.

Muddy Waters' record blared loudly over the chatter of the bar. I loved me some Muddy. Shooter's crooked smile was wide; he had his hand between my thighs and I didn't stop him. He was whispering something real nasty in my ear with his beer breath lightly grazing my neck.

Sallie pulled on my arm to get me away from him. "Sade, girl, we need to get you home before you get into some trouble."

"Take your goody two shoed hands off me! I'm not doing anything. Stop being a wet rag."

Shooter's hands were finding their way around the insides of my panties as I pushed my breasts up against his chest. He held me closer.

Sallie tapped me on the shoulder nervously. "I need you to listen to me, Sade... Your man is here."

"Get up off of me." I giggled, wrapping my arms around Shooter's neck. Before I knew it, Jerome was right there inside of the Texas Playhouse, and he was behind me, snatching me off that stool before I had a chance to get my act together.

To Shooter, Jerome bellowed roughly with his big hands balled up into tight fists. He was ready to knock him out if he had to. "I suggest you take your hands off my woman."

Shooter curled his top lip into a snarl. "The lady is with me, tonight. Go and get your own damned broad."

"Hey, watch your mouth. She belongs with me."

"You want to take this outside?" Shooter didn't back down as he took off his jacket.

"If you want to fight, the favor is in me."

"You fixin' to talk out of place." Shooter's whole body stiffened.

Jerome didn't back down. "I don't play de dozens. If you trynna jump salt, that's your ass."

Shooter took a good look at Jerome's muscular military build and realized he was too drunk to square off with him. He wasn't even sure if he could hold his gun steady enough to shoot him if he had to... might mess around and accidentally shoot himself. Shooter sat back down silently.

Niyah Moore

I giggled at the room because it was spinning around me so fast, I felt like I was on a carnival ride. For whatever reason, my brain wasn't telling me that I had just got caught pressed up in another man's sweaty arms.

Jerome's hand snatched me and he dug into my arm with such a force that it nearly snapped me back into reality. "Ouch."

"Sade, I'm taking you home right now!" Jerome shouted louder than the music.

The whole bar was staring by then.

"Baby, you're hurting my arm."

He eased up his grip a little, but not by much as he escorted me toward the entrance. When Jerome noticed I couldn't walk straight to the car without stumbling in my heels, he tossed me over his shoulder in one sweep. Once in the car, he buckled me in.

Sallie ran out of the Texas Playhouse behind us. "Jerome, can I get a ride home?"

"Yeah, come on."

"What you doing down here, J? I thought you had to work late," I mumbled, holding my spinning head. "You're being a real drag, you know that?"

"I did work late. I'm off now." He closed the passenger door and then went around to his side of the car and got in and drove away from in front of the Playhouse. "What were you two doing down there at this time, Sallie? I thought you were goin' to only stay for a little while. It's almost four in the damned morning."

"I was ready to leave, but she wanted to stay and there was no way I was gonna to let her stay up there alone with that jig."

"Awwwww shit, I was just having a lil' fun," I slurred.

MAJOR JAZZ

"… Who was that?" He scowled, staring over at me with his nostrils flaring.

"Who? Shooter? Aw, he ain't nobody," I giggled.

"Do you know him, Sallie?" He stared at her through his review mirror.

"Everybody knows Shooter… He's just a mug man who doesn't know how to control his trigger finger."

"Don't tell me she was 'bout to leave with that lame, was she?"

I interrupted their conversation, "Ugh, you two don't want me to have fun anymore. Just 'cause I'm hangin' out with you don't mean I can't still do what I want to do. I used to be so free before I met you."

"You want to break up?" Defeated tears were in his intense eyes. "Huh? Since, we're just hangin' out."

"We might as well." I rested my head up against the side window.

"She's talkin' reckless," Sallie interjected before I could say anything else stupid. "Let her pile up some Z's. In the morning, she'll be sorry. I'm sure she won't even remember this."

"Go to hell, Sal..." I groaned and moaned. Why couldn't my head stop from spinning?

We all ate our own individual silence until we dropped Sallie at home. I didn't budge. There was no way I was going to leave Jerome. I didn't want us to end that way.

"Are you coming in Sade?" she asked.

"No… I'm going home with J."

"Oh, alright… Good night, Jerome. Thanks for the ride."

"You're welcome. See you later." He watched her until she was safely inside the house. As soon as he pulled away from that curb, he uttered, "What I just seen at that bar… You had no business… After tonight,

Niyah Moore

we're through. You hear me? You can be as free as you want to be from now on."

"You don't mean that."

"How come I don't? I can't trust you to be faithful to me. Is that why you don't want to marry me?"

"I don't want to marry you 'cause I'm gonna get my kicks while I'm still young..." I had to catch my breath because the urge I had to throw up was coming and fast.

"Baby, pull over."

He took a double look at me to see that I was going to throw up, so he pulled over as quickly as he could, but I couldn't get the door opened fast enough before I tossed my cookies right there on the floor of his automobile.

"Aw, Sade. Not in the car."

"I'm sorry... I'm sorry..." I couldn't stop it. I was that sick.

He rolled down all the windows and tried to clean me up the best he could with extra towels he had in the trunk of the car. When we got to his house, he undressed me because my clothes had been ruined by my vomit. He put them in the bathtub to soak and helped me get into his comfortable bed. While I slept, he cleaned out his car.

I woke up the next morning feeling every bit hung over. He was sleeping without touching me. A pounding headache and the memory of him showing up came crashing down like a tidal wave. I slipped out of bed, careful not to wake him, brushed my teeth before climbing back into bed, and woke him with soft moist kisses... kisses as my apology.

He fluttered his eyelashes and stared up at me with a blank stare.

"Good morning," I said.

"Good morning..."

MAJOR JAZZ

"I feel really terrible."

He swallowed what looked like a hard lump in his throat. "I bet."

"My head is killing me. I'm never getting that drunk again."

He grunted; he was too disgusted to say anything else at that moment.

I kissed his lips, but his soft lips didn't return my kiss the way he usually did. He just stared at me as if I were some stranger. I knew what he was thinking. He fell in love with a wild woman and thought he was going to be able to change me overnight. The hurt in his eyes hit something deep down that had never been reached before. To make a change to love him the way he needed to be loved because he deserved that much from me, was something I needed to do. If I couldn't give it to him, then I was going to have to move on. There was no way I wanted to move on without him because I truly loved him.

"I'll marry you, J."

He didn't blink or show any sort of emotion, just kept staring.

"Did you hear me? I said I'll marry you."

"…I heard you."

"I want to be your wife."

Silence from him.

"We can get married today if you want. I'm ready. I don't want to live my life this way. I don't want to imagine my life without you."

He took hold of my face and squeezed my cheeks between his thumb and forefinger, so he could stare into me. "Don't you dare say that to me out of your guilty conscious, you hear me?"

Tears emerged instantly, my heart was pounding, and my brain was racing at the thought that this would be our last night together. "I swear to you, Jerome. I mean it. I love you."

"I'm searching for *real* love… Don't do this out of pity for me…"

"I don't pity you. I love you. I want to marry you as soon as possible."

He let go of my face, shaking his head slowly at my shamed face. "I will marry you, but only if you truly mean it. What you exhibited last night didn't make me feel like you are being sincere with me."

"I'm being sincere. Let's just get married."

He held me close to him, as close as I could be, with his heart hammering against my cheek. I closed my eyes and felt it in the depth of my soul. He was more than perfect for me. The fear I had of letting go of my old ways dissipated and I embraced his love with a fresh face.

Sallie

The front door opened, cold air bum rushed its way inside, and when it slammed, it startled Mother Dear, Father, and I. Our aunts had ended their visit early that morning to go back to the Philippines and Sade was out shopping with Jerome, so it was either Lucille or Johnnie acting a fool and taking their anger out on the door.

"Who is that slammin' that front door?" Mother Dear shouted.

"Has Johnnie been home, yet?" Lucille panicked as she stormed through the house, searching for him.

"No," I replied while pressing the hair lining Mother Dear's neck in the kitchen.

Father was at the dinning table eating some leftover chicken adobe. He always ate alone since he was always the last one home after closing the cleaners. He didn't answer as he looked up from his newspaper and Mother Dear held her head still while I moved the pressing comb carefully so I wouldn't burn her.

"I haven't seen him. Did he come home last night?" Mother Dear asked with her chin into her chest.

"No, he stayed out all night. I was hoping he would've been back by now." Lucille drew in a deep breath as tears clouded her eyes.

I observed the way Lu was rubbing her stomach. It had grown into a round ball. Did this woman think we couldn't see her midsection growing so? I held my tongue from shouting at her because I knew it would only upset our parents to fight with her over the obvious problem. She was pregnant and her husband was a creep. Mother Dear pretended not to notice by keeping her eyes on the ground.

Lucille stormed out of the kitchen and into her bedroom, still looking for Johnnie. It was no use, he hadn't been home. Her loud sobs echoed down the hall to the kitchen and it prompted me to leave Mother Dear and the pressing comb. Before I could reach her door, she slammed it because she saw me coming. I knew what she always feared when it came to Johnnie. Usually, if he didn't come home for a few days, he was most likely in jail.

I knocked on her door. To my surprise she opened right up and extended her arms for me to hug her. Her round stomach met me first, and I held her close. I didn't know if it was just my imagination, but it felt like the baby kicked me. I didn't act startled by it. Lu needed me. Though crass words wanted to fly from my lips, she didn't need to hear any of them.

Caressing the long hair that was flowing down her back, I whispered in her ear, "Everything will get better."

"What if he's in jail again?"

I kept quiet so our parents wouldn't hear our conversation. "We have some work to do... for that sweet little baby growing inside of you... Please, don't worry or stress. We wouldn't want you to loose *him* too."

She stared at me as if she were surprised that I knew and could say anything so nice about it. "Thank you sis... I think it's a boy too."

Suddenly, the front door flew open, and Johnnie strolled in as if he hadn't been gone all night, as if he owned the right not to check in with his wife. Lucille and I stared at him from the hallway while Mother Dear and Father looked at him as if he'd lost his mind.

Niyah Moore

"Good afternoon." He smiled and gave Lucille a wink.

"I would feel much better if your sorry ass was in jail!" Lucille stormed back into the bedroom and slammed the door while Johnnie just laughed and headed to the bathroom to wash the woman he had been laying with off his body.

Sade

Two nights before my wedding, Jerome's sailor friends threw him a bachelor party at Bop City. Those sailors drank almost all night while listening to Major's band jam. My sisters threw a classy party for me at my parents' house. We had some wine, food, bridal games, and gifts. With a host of close friends and my mother's family, we had a good 'ole time. I couldn't wait to be Mrs. Hanes.

"So, Jerome is really gonna make you his wife?" Lucille asked while helping herself to a second round of the buffet of ham, candied yams, string beans, catfish, macaroni and cheese, and potato salad prepared by Mother Dear and her sisters.

"Yes, he is." I flashed the ring in her face to remind her.

"He must be crazy." Lucille laughed, trying to still conceal her pregnant tummy with an oversized sweater.

"Why he gotta be crazy?" Sallie scowled.

"We all know Sade don't know how to be a wife."

"Lucille," Mother Dear hissed, wagging her finger. "Don't start that nonsense tonight. You should be happy for your sister. We are all here to celebrate her."

"I'm happy for her, Mother Dear. I just feel sorry for him, that's all."

"Lucille!"

"Mother Dear," I said, "everything is fine. Lu Lu isn't bugging me one bit. I know that I'm gonna try to be the best wife I can be. I'm gonna make mistakes 'cause I'm human and Jerome loves me regardless 'cause that's what real men do."

"Well then, honey, you have yourself a real man," Aunt Henrietta said.

Lucille rolled her eyes as she scooped a big helping of potato salad onto her paper plate. The more she denied being pregnant, seemed like the bigger she was getting and everyone whispered about it behind her back the whole party.

"When you gonna open up these presents?" Sallie quizzed while eyeballing the beautifully wrapped gifts.

I sat on the sofa. "I'm ready now. Pass me the first one."

Sallie clapped. "Okay, everyone, Sade is getting ready to open her gifts… Here, open mine first."

Hers was wrapped in silver and white paper. I carefully made sure not to tear the pretty paper.

"Chile, that's only paper. Rip that mess off," Sallie exclaimed.

I ignored her. It truly was too pretty to just rip off. I opened the box and inside was a pretty white nightgown trimmed in lace. It was gorgeous. The ladies chattered with sounds of approval.

"Sallie, this is nice. Thank you."

"You should wear it on your wedding night."

Mother Dear said over the chatter, "Since I'm the mother of the bride to be, I think you should open mines next." She handed me a pink wrapped box. It was the largest in the pile.

After taking the paper off and opening the box, I gasped. It was the wedding gown I wanted, but couldn't afford. "Mother Dear, how'd you get this?"

"Your father would do anything for you. Do you like it?"

Niyah Moore

I hopped up to hug her tight. "Thank you so much, Mother Dear. I love it."

"Well, how in the hell are we supposed to follow Lillian's gift?" Aunt Henrietta complained with her hands resting on her big wide hips. One thing was for certain and that was my mother's sisters were all blessed with heavy shapely bottoms.

Everyone in the house laughed at her. The smile on Mother Dear's face was the biggest I had seen in a very long time. Joy filled me up on that alone. My bash ended pretty late in the evening. My sisters, Mother Dear, and I had the house almost cleaned close to midnight. Before we could get into bed, there was a knock on the front door.

"Who's expecting company at this time of night?" Mother Dear asked.

I shrugged while Lucille and Sallie looked just as confused. "I'll get the door." I opened the door and a SFPD officer was standing there. With a deep frown I asked, "Yes?"

"Hello ma'am. Are you Sade Aquino?"

"Yes, I'm Sade Aquino..."

"My name is John Sumter and I'm with the San Francisco Police Department. There has been an accident tonight..."

Lucille came behind me and opened the door wider. "Is this about Johnnie?"

Johnnie hadn't made it home yet, but they asked for me, not her. "No, ma'am..."

"What kind of accident?" Lucille barked over him before he could get out another word.

"Jerome Hanes was involved in a motor vehicle accident this evening. His motor vehicle collided with a utility pole over on Golden Gate."

"Oh my..." Sallie gasped.

MAJOR JAZZ

"Is he alright?" Mother Dear queried.

"Where is he now?" Lucille questioned.

My ears waited for his answer as my heart raced in fear. Though, I couldn't speak, I knew what the outcome was. I knew why the boys in blue were on our porch. The pain in my stomach told me this news wasn't good at all.

"He was pronounced dead at the scene."

My heart dropped and so did I. The pit of my stomach felt as if someone just ran me over with a truck. I knew he was going to say it before he said it. Sallie knelt with me as I cried.

Lucille pressed, "Are you sure it was him?"

"He had his driver's license on him. One of his friends was there when we got there. He identified his body."

I covered my mouth with both hands as tears clouded my vision. "My fiancé is dead?"

"Yes ma'am. Does he have any other family that you could contact and let them know?"

"No, no, no, no..."

"All of his family lives in New Jersey..." Lucille spoke for me while I cried in Sallie's arms. "They were on their way down for their wedding. They were supposed to get married in two days."

The officer cleared his throat before he said, "I'm truly sorry about all of this. It appears he had been drinking quite a bit. He lost control of the car while driving too fast. He wasn't wearing a safety belt and went right through the front windshield. His body is on the way to General Hospital. You can contact them to make arrangements with the family for a funeral."

I heard him, but I didn't want to hear him. I felt as if I were going to die with him. Jerome wasn't supposed to leave this earth that way. Good guys weren't supposed to die suddenly, but he did. I can not explain in words how much pain I felt when those seconds turned to minutes, minutes into hours, hours into days, and days into months. The pain never left me.

To be honest, I never got over him and I dated plenty of men years later, but I never married another. I know that my heart broke when he died in that car crash, but I poured the mended pieces into the one thing I am forever grateful for, our son.

Lyric's House

He had a heavy flow…

Due to his bottomless love for poignant words, he spoke powerfully over microphones throughout our neighborhood in the Western Addition of San Francisco. When he opened up his charming mouth, he commanded everyone's full attention. His hard-edged demeanor was much like a young man lingering the ghetto streets, cruising for a bruising, yet his particular style of dress was classic… always in a nice pair of slacks. You see, that's what separated him from the hoodlums.

His skin was smooth, the color between hot café au laits and delicious mochas. Those dark brown eyes of his carried a curious mystery, maybe a little hurt, retribution, and pain stemming from his childhood. I wasn't sure what his story was in the beginning; however, he was the epitome of what my man was supposed to look like. Naturally thick and wavy hair was combed and cut to perfection, not a strand out of place… such a pretty Negro. Just saying he was a divine specimen was an understatement. Besides, he wasn't only fine; he was incredible.

The nascent tenderness he revealed echoed through his hypnotizing heaven sent lyrics and encouraged me to keep writing myself, though I wasn't on his level of sophistication. I was a beginner. I wrote songs and sang all while trying to find the courage to make my way onto a stage back then. I was seventeen years old and too petrified to showcase my natural unforced talent, so I sang my ballads in the bathtub. Needless to say, the bathroom walls were my audience.

Our common thing, writing, drew us together in a way that electrified me; only he didn't know it just yet. He didn't even know I was alive until one glorious early summer morning of 1951. As I was preparing to leave my father's barbecue joint, the man with the heavy flow wasn't watching where he was going while he loud mouthed someone else outside of the restaurant. "Hey, I'll see you later, jive ass motherfucker!"

I tried to get out of his way, but his arm knocked my two school books and notebook to the floor. "Oh... excuse me." He seemed genuinely concerned as he quickly picked up my loose papers.

I froze because it was *him*. I couldn't believe Ali Watson was in my daddy's restaurant. We hadn't formally met, so the lucky girl inside of me squealed inaudibly.

His eyes...

Those sparkling brown eyes lit up once he realized he had sheets of my music in his hands. "You're a singer, musician, or something?"

I wanted him to look at me.

Finally, once he was done gaping at my sheet music, his eyes met mine, and it felt like the gates of heaven opened up while the angels sang just for me. Feeling my knees buckle, I locked them in place to hold myself up. A look of what I thought love would look like nestled under his long gaze. I mean, I hadn't experienced love on any level before, so I had no clue, but that must've been what a man looked like when he was in love at first sight.

I didn't think I could speak, but to my amazement, I replied, "I sing... not professionally or nothing. Just for a blast. I write music. You play?"

Niyah Moore

Eyes still sparkling, he replied, "I wish I could. Shoot, I would jam everyday if I could. I write, well, not music though... poems, articles, and things of that nature. When can I hear you sing?"

My brown eyes, too, twinkled like stars in the pitch black sky. "My daddy might let me sing my songs here soon. He owns the place and-"

"You Earl Taylor's daughter?" he interrupted while picking up my books next.

"Yes..."

His huge white handsome grin entranced me. "I dig that. My name is Ali Watson. What's yours, lovely lady?"

"Her name is Kae." My father's voice stopped our eyes from making passionate love to one another. My daddy's stern look at the young man made me clear my own throat and look away. "How can I help you, young man?"

Ali placed the books back into my arms, smiling at my dad respectfully. "Good morning, Mr. Taylor. I actually came down here to speak with you about a potential set... A poetry set."

My daddy came around from the service counter and stood in front of us. "Well, I'll be at the Texas Playhouse later this evening. Come have a drink with me and my wife and we'll talk business. You old enough to drink, ain't you?"

"Yes sir. I just made twenty-one."

I lowered my head, placed my eyes on the multi-colored tiled floor, and felt sad about not being old enough because I really wanted to go to the Texas Playhouse with them. On occasion, I snuck down there, but only if I knew my parents were going to be home sleeping.

"Get on to school, Kae," my dad said gently.

MAJOR JAZZ

"Okay…" I tried to stall to be in Ali's presence a little longer. "I'm making dinner tonight."

"Alright, when you get home, tell your mama to meet me at the Playhouse this evening."

"Yes, sir. See you later, Daddy."

I didn't give my eyes back to Ali while leaving 'cause Daddy would know that I had a secret crush. With his overbearing, strict rules, that was unacceptable. I wasn't allowed to date, let alone look at another man while in his presence.

As I walked down Fillmore Street to cross Post, I clutched my books close to my zooming heart, shivered a bit under the sun's rays, though it wasn't the bay's breeze that caused the chill. Ali had given me goose bumps. It was as if, at that moment, a spotlight was shining on us in a pitch-black room and nobody was there but the two of us. Some bizarre foreign feeling was upon me -- the kind that felt like it wasn't going to wash away easily, I could tell. Wobbly knees took over the entire two blocks I walked to catch the 22 bus on time.

Kae Taylor

I couldn't wait to get home from what seemed like one of the longest days of summer and there were only a few weeks of school left until graduation. The lovesick matter of my mind wouldn't let me focus on schoolwork alone. Ali's eyes had given my heartstrings a new strum and writing a song was all I could think about. Time on the clock seemed as if it slowed down, but as soon as school was over, I rushed home, washed up in the bathroom, got out of my school attire, and changed into a loose pair of pants and shirt.

I went into my parents' bedroom before heading down to the kitchen to get started on the meatloaf, potatoes, and peas I had planned to prepare. My mama was standing in front of the body length oval mirror in her bra, panty, and girdle as she held her stockings up against the lamp looking for runs. Her sweet womanly perfume greeted me first before I could take a good look at her pretty dolled up face.

"Hi, Mama… Daddy wants you to meet him at the Texas Playhouse after dinner."

"I know it," she replied in her southern drawl. "He called, so don't make dinner for us 'cause we stayin' out late tonight. We might eat ova at Elsie's Nook. Look like it's gonna be one of those nights."

Beaumont, Texas was where my parents were both born and raised. They moved to San Francisco because the shipyard hired men from all over and paid well during the start of World War II. That was daddy's first job in the city before he opened up Earl's Barbecue Joint, home of real Texas-style glazed ribs.

Whenever they left me at home alone on Friday nights, I was supposed to do the same things I did when they were home. I studied, wrote songs, and listened to some records with my best friend, Georgia. She lived next door and was closer to eighteen years old than I was, had the smoothest looking dark skin I had ever seen with one dimple in her left cheek, and a picture perfect smile to go with it. Whenever our parents stayed out late, we would sneak down somewhere and listen to some live music for a little while. Then, we would get in the bed before their return.

"How long y'all plan on being gone?"

See, I was calculating. I needed to know exactly how long they would be out to plan the great escape so we wouldn't get caught.

"You know how your daddy gets when he's drinkin' scotch and soda. We may be out all night."

"What should I do about dinner? Is Daddy bringin' food home?"

"Not tonight. Why don't you make one of them Swanson's turkey pot pies I got in there?"

I immediately frowned, but she couldn't see my face. She was too busy getting ready. She bought those ghastly oven dinners for nights like these. I would've preferred to cook a meatloaf, but with Mama, her suggestions were always orders. I wasn't going to give her any lip.

"Can Georgia stay over?"

"If her parents say it's fine."

Georgia's parents were easy-going. They stayed out to party all the time with little to no instructions. Their one and only rule was to keep the house clean. With a house full with four brothers and four sisters, Georgia was smack dab in the middle. Some of the older ones looked after the smaller ones and kept the house clean anyway, so she didn't have much to worry over.

Mama eased her nude colored stockings over her smooth caramelized legs. As a woman, she took care of her personal appearance and taught me the same way. My eyes drifted over to her green chiffon party dress and pearls out on the bed. I loved that dress. It fit her curves like a glove.

Daddy thanked God every time she put it on. "Lola," he would say, "bring your fine behind on ova' here. Give me some suga. The Lord knew what he was doin' when he blessed me with you."

She would giggle with a smile so bright. "Now, Earl, you cut that out. We have a bash to go to."

The adoring passion they displayed was admirable. One day, I hope to have that, too.

"Your brother comes home soon, I believe. The Navy letting him get some free time before he go back." Deep lines penetrated her forehead. She worried about Earl Jr., even though World War II had been over since '45. Another war, The Cold War was going on and she wanted her only son home from Korea in one piece.

"I can't wait to see him. He tells me he's in love."

Mama smacked her full lips after taking a sip of room temperature tap water from a glass on the dresser, and then shook her head as she maneuvered her half slip past her hips. "Humph... He don't know that girl and don't know what love is. I keep tellin' him he got plenty of time to fall in love. Here, Kae, help me zip this dress up." She pulled the green dress up over her round behind.

As soon as it was all the way up, I zipped it. "There you go, Mama. Are you wearing that curly wig?"

"Naw, I got a new one. Get it out the closet for me. It's at the top in a plastic bag."

I opened the closet and pulled it down. Mama always purchased the brown short cropped wigs. They looked nice on her slender oval face. She preferred wigs because her hair was too thin to hold a good style.

"I gotta finish up now, so go 'head and heat that pie up."

"Yes ma'am."

Even though I wasn't fooling with that turkey pot pie, I went downstairs and turned the oven on anyway before calling Georgia. I had a few extra dollars in my piggy bank and was going to get something else to eat when the coast was clear.

She picked up the line after a few rings, "Hello." In her background, I could hear a loud commotion. It was always so noisy at her house like a party was going on. If it wasn't her parents fussing at the kids or one another, her siblings were.

"It's me… Kae… What you doin' tonight?"

She blew air out of her lips before she yelled into the background, "Can't y'all see I'm on the damned phone? Shut the hell up! Hello…"

"I'm here…"

"They are so rude… Now, what you ask me?"

"What you doin' tonight?" I bit on what was left of my nail. I had a bad habit of chewing at my nails, so much they never had the chance to grow pretty.

"All I know is I'm trynna get out this zoo I call my house. If I don't get out, I'm gonna kill one of 'em. What you doin'?"

"I'm sitting here, heating up this frozen mess again. Mama is getting ready to leave now to meet Daddy down over at the Texas Playhouse."

"My folks just left for The Blue Mirror, so you know what that means. They ain't comin' home 'til the wee hours of the mornin'."

"My mama said you can come over."

"I'm on my way. You wanna go to Bop City?"

"Shhhh… I won't say over this line. Come on."

"Okay. Bye."

"Bye."

I hung up the black rotary phone and contained my excitement while I took the pot pie out of the freezer, unwrapped the packaging, and put it on a baking pan. Once in the oven, I set the timer to remind me to take it out.

Mama's black peep toe pumps that strapped around her ankles clicked down the wooden stairs as she called from the front door, "I'm outta here. 'Night lil' girl."

I stood in the entryway of the kitchen admiring her glamour. Pearls always went well with that dress. "Good night. Have fun."

"How does my wig look?" She patted it with two hands and smiled proudly. "Is it crooked?"

"Naw, it looks good as always."

"Thank you. Don't let that pie burn up. You hear me?"

"Yes ma'am. Kiss Daddy for me."

"I will." She winked, went out of the door, strutting in her mink stole and small black crocodile clutch in her hand.

As soon as she drove away, I put on a Billie Holiday record I purchased from Melrose Record Shop while I waited for Georgia.

I sang along, *"It cost me a lot…*
But there's one thing that I've got…
It's my man…

MAJOR JAZZ

It's my man..."

My Man was one of my favorite Billie Holiday recordings to sing. I would've died at the chance to meet her. She had been down to Blackshear's Café Society a few times, and on occasion, she sang in a few "whites only" clubs downtown, but I hadn't seen her.

I tapped a pencil on my notepad before earnest lyrics about *his* eyes flowed through me. A love song so deep overflowed onto the blank sheet of paper. A harmonic melody came from the unknown -- a place I couldn't explain -- a gift from God.

Georgia didn't knock or ring the bell. She never did. She walked in with her "going out clothes", a blue pencil skirt and white blouse, tucked under her arm. "You in here singing those blues again? Honey, I swear, you sound better than Lady Day. When you gonna get your scary tail up on stage?"

I snickered 'cause it was the truth. I was scary. "Soon... I'm just waiting on the right opportunity to do so."

She flashed me a pack of Lucky Strikes. "Look what I got, stole 'em from Ed. He's gonna pick us up in that hunk of junk he just purchased, so let's hurry and get dressed."

Ed was her boyfriend and he smoked like a chimney. Ever since she lost her virginity in the back seat of his folks' car, he didn't let her go too far out of his sight, but she always managed to steal cigarettes from him. I couldn't stand smoking 'cause it made me cough so bad, but they made me feel grown up.

"Where you want to go?" I questioned.

"We goin' to Bop City, of course. Jam session is always a gas. Maybe you can jump on stage."

Niyah Moore

"Shoot... Not on that stage... I'll get on any stage but that one. You seen how the crowd waves off the bad people when they don't like 'em."

"You won't get waved off 'cause you're not bad. Trust me, they'll love you."

I bit on the inside of my cheek while in thought. I dreamt of getting on that stage. The house band played and I sang fearlessly. If only my nerves didn't get the best of me, my dream would become a reality.

Right when we were about to head up the stairs to get dressed, someone buzzed the bell.

"Damn, that nigger 'sho drive fast," Georgia fussed. "I told him to hold off 'til we were ready. He must want to get cursed out." She snatched the door open with her hand sitting on her hip. Her frown quickly dissipated once she realized it wasn't Ed, but a handsome stranger. "Well, hello there."

"Good evening. Is Kae here?"

His voice...

I knew who that voice belonged to before I could see him. My heart skipped a beat.

"She's right here." Georgia smiled at me. She knew all about my crush on him and opened the door wider to reveal all of him.

"Ali?" I didn't want to frown too hard as if I weren't happy to see him, so I smiled instead.

"Good evening, Kae. I hope I'm not disturbing you."

He was nicely dressed in black slacks, a white dress shirt, and shiny shoes. His cologne was strong, but smelled the way a man's should. To think he got dressed up to see me had me blushing.

I pat my bangs in place. "Good evening... What are you doin' here?"

"I'm here to take you out. I got permission from your father. How long will it take you to get ready?"

I wasn't sure if I believed that he asked the right man. My daddy wasn't one to persuade easily. "He did? When you ask him?"

"Just a few minutes ago, over at Wes's place."

"...Was he drunk?"

"Barely." He winked. "But, he did have quite a few scotches and sodas in him."

"Hmmm..." I wasn't so sure. My suspicion was up, but I played along with him because the thought was nice.

"You ladies have plans this evening?"

Georgia beat me to answering. "My boyfriend is on his way so we can go get some food and then head on over to Bop City. You should come along. By the way, I'm Georgia."

"It's nice to meet you, Georgia." His eyes were back on me. "I'll come as long as Miss Kae says its fine."

I giggled, making my eyes dance between his and Georgia's. "That's alright with me. Come in and sit on the couch. We'll be right down."

He stepped inside and closed the door behind him. While he sat on my parents' sofa, we ran up the stairs to get dressed quickly.

"What you gonna to wear?" Georgia questioned once my bedroom door was closed.

"Should I wear the poodle skirt, white blouse, and sweater?"

"You better not wear that poodle skirt to the club! Honey, then they'll know you just a lil' girl." Georgia pulled at the clothes in my closet until she found something that caught her eye. "Here, put this on." She handed me the forbidden black dress.

Niyah Moore

"I've only worn this dress once and my daddy says it's too short. He would die if he even knew it's still in my closet."

"Well your daddy ain't here." Georgia clapped her hands happily as she removed her shirt. "Ali is a classy guy. I can tell his heart is eighteen karat."

I tossed my clothes to the floor and fell back on the bed with my hand on chest. "That's why my heart is burning so."

"Stop goofin'. Ed will be here in second. Wear those heels you got from GallenKamp's."

I laughed at my own silliness and dressed as fast as I could. I put on a cotton button up sweater to protect me from the night's chilly air. We both fixed our bobbed hair, put on a little rouge on our cheeks and lips from my mama's dresser. Georgia liked to stuff her bra with tissue. I didn't need stuffing; I was pretty stacked.

Ed honked the horn from outside. Georgia rolled her eyes as she pulled back the curtain to stare out of my parents' bedroom window. "Daddy-O is tootin' that thang like nobody can hear him. Ed can be a real crumb sometimes."

I laughed at her slick talk about her man. That was the reason why she liked him so much. His rudeness captured her heart ever since we started high school.

When we made our way downstairs, Ali stood up. I could tell by the look in his glittering eyes that he was impressed at how grown up I looked. I tried to mask my smile behind my hand while I hurried past him in the kitchen to take that horrible pot pie out of the oven. The timer hadn't gone off yet, but I didn't want the house to burn down. I shut the oven off and grabbed a pot holder.

MAJOR JAZZ

He kept staring into the kitchen after me. My cheeks grew hot and my smile was wide.

Ed honked again.

Georgia yelled as she walked down the porch steps, "Cool it, baby!"

I locked up the house and tossed the key inside my little coin purse.

Ed shouted at Georgia from the car, "Hurry up!"

"Don't rush me, fool. Can't you see me comin'?" Her voice was so loud it was echoing in the night's crisp air.

"I see you, but you ain't moving fast enough."

"You sure you want to ride with them?" Ali questioned with his eyebrows pointing slightly down into a frown.

"Don't pay 'em any mind. That's how they talk to one another…"

"Well, dig this… I'm thinking you and I can walk down to Jackson's for some good 'ole Creole food. Bop City is right 'round the corner from there. I'm sure Georgia won't mind."

Since we lived on Laguna and Geary, the walk was only about two blocks. I bit on my lower lip to prevent myself from biting my nails. Once at the bottom of the stairs, I still hadn't answered because my nervousness was getting in the way.

"Get yo' ass in this car!"

"Shut yo' ass up, Ed! Come on Kae, you comin'?" She was standing at the car by that time.

I really wasn't in the mood to hear those two go at it. I shook my head and replied, "We'll meet you at Bop City in a lil' bit."

Georgia shrugged, hopped into Ed's brand new Cadillac, and as soon as the door was closed, he pulled away from the curb in a reckless manner.

Niyah Moore

I didn't really know what she seen in that yella knucklehead, other than his family's inherited money. His wealthy family was from down south somewhere. They owned the 115-room Ellis Hotel with a lobby and cocktail lounge on Ellis Street.

"You look really nice," Ali complimented.

"Thank you. You always look nice."

He tipped his hat towards me. "Do I always? I just met you this morning."

"I've seen you around and at the Ellis Theater and at the pool hall, here and there, with your friends."

"You heard me recite at the theater?"

"Yes."

"So, you're familiar with my writing?"

"Yes and quite frankly, I enjoy it."

"One day, I plan to be published... Say, do you think you'd be able to turn one into a song?"

I hadn't thought about turning poetry into songs, but I figured it wouldn't be hard to do. Words were words, just arranged differently. "I guess I could."

"I can bring over some of my poetry and we can try it out. How does that sound?"

"Sounds like a blast."

"If it comes out nice, I think you should sing it for Major."

"Major Ingram?" I nearly stuttered.

"Yes, Major Ingram." He chuckled at my wide curious eyes.

Major Ingram was Fillmore's best pianist. I saw him at Bop City a few times when he was on that small stage doing his thing. Whew, that boy had talent. He banged those keys so hard his wavy hair always went wild.

"You know Major Ingram personally?" I asked in awe.

MAJOR JAZZ

"We grew up together over on Buchanan. He's looking for a singer. I have a feeling that you'll do real well with him."

"You haven't heard me sing before... How do you know I'm any good at it?"

He examined me from head to toe as we crossed the intersection. He made sure no oncoming cars were coming as we strolled. "I can tell. You have the sweetest little voice when you talk. Major will love your voice."

"... Major Ingram is out of this world. He plays those keys like nobody I know. Everyone loves him around here."

That was the truth. He was the neighborhood's celebrity.

"I can introduce you tonight, if you like. He's always at Bop City."

I hesitated. "Um... Tonight?"

"Tonight."

Fear struck my heart. The moment I dreaded was possibly upon me as stage fright pulled me. "Will he ask me to get on stage?"

"He may."

"No, no, no... *I can't*... I'm not ready for Bop City." My hands began to shake. I clasped them together to stop myself from trembling.

As soon as we were on the sidewalk, he stopped me gently with the softest touch of his hand on top of mine. He stared into my soul with his piercing eyes. "Tonight, your dreams will come true. When you get up there, just close your eyes and imagine no one is there but you. Sing your little heart out just like you do in your bathroom. Can you do that for me?"

"How do you know I sing in my bathroom?"

Niyah Moore

A handsome smile branded his face, knowingly. Maybe all singers sang in the bathtub, I thought. I swallowed hard and got lost in the intensity of his magnetic stare. Underneath his magical spell, I felt this tingly sensation creep up the back of my neck, and instantly, I felt all stage fright leave my floating body as the tiny hairs stood straight up all over me. "What am I going to sing?"

"Sing whatever you like. He can play anything."

My scattered mind raced. What song would I sing? It was a once in a lifetime opportunity. Billie? Bessie? "Oh, I can sing Dinah Washington's *Please Send Me Somebody to Love.*"

He winked before lifting my chin to see my eyes again. "I bet you can make that ballad out real nice."

"I'll try my best."

After another block to Post, we took a right on Buchanan. We entered the Creole-owned restaurant, Jackson's Nook. Ali opened the door for me. It was crowded, but he managed to find us a table for two in the far corner. He tipped his hat toward smiley-faced women and slid some skin to brothers he knew. Ali worked the room as if he were the person everybody was waiting for.

He pulled out a chair for me, I sat, and then he sat across from me.

"What are your plans after high school?"

"Well, my daddy wants me to enroll in the nursing program, but I really don't want to."

"That's not a bad suggestion, but what does Kae want to be when she grows up?"

I hadn't shared my dreams with anyone other than Georgia. I wasn't sure if I should've shared my dream with him because I didn't want him to think I was just a little girl. Needless to say, his eyes encouraged me.

"As silly as this may sound, I want to be a famous singer, make records, and travel the world."

His grin was back to being wide. "That sounds good to me."

To have his support meant so much, even then.

"What about you? What's it that you do other than write and recite poetry?"

"I'm a busboy at Topsy's Roost part-time and a student at San Francisco State University. By the end of the summer, I'll have my Bachelor's degree in Journalism."

My ears perked up. "That's a big accomplishment. Your parents must be proud."

He paused as if his past was surfacing more quickly than he had liked it to. His eyes looked uneasy for a split second. "My parents are dead."

I immediately apologized with my right hand over my heart. "I'm so sorry. I didn't know."

He put his hand up to let me know it was fine. "It's okay. My parents died in a house fire when I was a kid. My mother's parents raised me in this neighborhood… instilled good things. I still stay with my grandmother, just until I'm done with school. Hopefully, I'll be able to rent a room around here."

Even though he wore a handsome smile, his eyes told it all. I could tell he yearned to know what kind of man his father was and what kind of scent his mother wore. Why wouldn't he yearn to know those things?

I bit on my lower lip and picked up the small menu that was pre-placed on the table. I really didn't know what else to say… felt like sticking a sock in my mouth.

Niyah Moore

"You should try their Jambalaya," he suggested. "It's the best I've ever had."

"I'll have that." I beamed, feeling relieved that I hadn't killed the mood between us.

"You have the most amazing smile I've ever seen."

He had a bad habit of making me blush. "Thank you. Your smile is amazing, too."

"You have a boyfriend?"

I shook my head. "No... My daddy is too overprotective for me to get close to anyone. He wants me to stay focused on school. I'm actually very surprised he let you take me out."

He leaned in close to me with his face turning real serious. "I have a confession. I asked your father if I could take you out tonight, but... he said no, nicely."

My eyes grew big and mouth flew wide open. "Now, how do you expect for Earl Taylor to ever let you take me out after this? What if we get caught together?"

"I'm willing to take that chance, for you... for your heart. To hear your voice, your giggle, and to just see your smile makes the risk all worthwhile. Would you have gone out with me if I told you the truth?"

"I'm not sure... You said he was okay with taking me out and I really believed you. I've never snuck around behind his back before..."

"That's not the complete truth. You were going to sneak out with Georgia tonight. Do you always sneak out when your folks are gone?"

I frowned and then giggled once I realized that I was busted. "Georgia and I never get caught, but we have to be careful if you want to see me again."

A waitress came to the table.

"Hello, Mary. How are you this fine evening?"

"I'm doing just fine, Ali. What can I get for you and Miss Kae?"

"We'll take two plates of that smokin' Jambalaya and two cokes."

"You got it comin' right your way." Mary winked before going to the kitchen to put in the order.

"How you know Miss Mary?" I asked.

"Mary is a real good friend of my family. She's such a sweet lady."

"Yes, she is. She's real good friends with my parents."

He smiled and paused before he said, "When we finish up here, we'll go around this corner and see what you got at Bop City."

I took a deep breath and exhaled. My nervousness came back to unsettle inside of me. What if I messed up or forgot the lyrics to the song? What if I tripped going on the stage? What if I tripped going off the stage? What if that horrible crowd waved me off? What if I hit a bad note? All those crazy thoughts began to nibble at me.

"You'll be fine," he said to reassure me.

All I could do was pray silently.

***

Bop City was filling up in that small narrow tight space, but it usually didn't get real crowded until around two in the morning. It was only slightly past ten, but it was still filled up pretty nice. The first couple of musicians to jump on stage were average players and you could tell they were still practicing their craft with all the bad riffs they hit. Jim, the owner, let anyone with an instrument jump on stage, as long as the audience agreed with them.

Georgia and Ed strolled in a little after us and joined us at our table. Georgia's hair looked a little out of place, as if she and Ed had already done some necking in the back seat of his car.

She wore a wicked smile that told she had. "You guys eat yet?"

"We ate at Jackson's Nook. Where'd y'all go?"

"Nowhere! See, that's where we should've gone." She hit Ed in the chest roughly. "I'm starvin'."

"So, order somethin' from here. They got a menu," Ed growled right back.

"All they got is fried chicken baskets and I don't want no chicken, Ed," Georgia blew air from her lips and stared at me. "How's everything goin' on your first date?"

I smiled and looked over at Ali to see if he could hear us, but he was too busy looking around the room. "Everything is solid."

"There goes Major." Ali eased out of his chair. "I'll be right back. Sit tight."

My stomach immediately tensed up and it felt like insects were crawling around inside.

Ali and Major greeted one another, like long time buddies who hadn't seen each other in a while. Even from a distance, Major was a looker in those suspenders and slacks. His light brown skin, wavy hair, and clean shaven face made all the women in the room swoon and fan themselves. There wasn't a woman in the house that didn't think Major was gorgeous. Next thing I knew, Ali and Major were heading to our table.

"Is that Major Ingram headin' our way?" Georgia asked, nudging me with her elbow.

"Looks that way…"

She immediately started straightening out her hair to make sure she looked decent. Ed flashed a look as if to tell her to watch herself. She rolled her eyes at him and kept right on.

MAJOR JAZZ

"Major, I want you to meet the most talented singer around, Kae Taylor." It was funny of him to introduce me that way when he hadn't heard me sing anything yet. "Kae, this is my friend, the talented pianist, Major Ingram."

Major had the lightest hazel eyes I'd ever seen on a black person and I couldn't help but stare as he spoke with that gold tooth shining in the corner of his mouth. "It's a pleasure to meet you, Kae. You ready to sing tonight?"

I smiled and nodded, though my stage fright had kicked in full blast. I felt like shaking my head and screaming *No!*

"You're singin' tonight?" Georgia asked with wide excited eyes.

"She's singin' with the band in just a few minutes." Ali smiled confidently as Major headed toward the stage.

"You... tell him what song?" I questioned with fret building a nest in my stomach.

"Calm down, Kae. I told him which song and he's getting ready now," Ali said.

Georgia asked, "Why didn't you tell me you were gonna sing?"

"Kind of just happened on the way here."

I bit on my lower lip and went over the lyrics in my head as my heart began to race even faster. For some reason, I couldn't remember the first line of the song and felt like I was going to pass out, so I fanned myself a bit.

"Are you okay?" Ali observed.

"Um, do you think you can get me a glass of water?"

"I sure can." He went over to one of the waitresses to request a glass for me.

Niyah Moore

Felt like my heart was going to pound out of my chest. I grabbed it to make sure it was still inside of me.

Georgia clapped her hands, but then stopped when she noticed I wasn't quite as jazzed as she was. I was beginning to sweat bullets. "Just take a few deep breaths, Kae."

I inhaled slowly and exhaled while I watched Major tell the bass, sax, and drummer what song to play. It was too late to change my wavering mind because the band was preparing. Major slid coolly onto the piano stool and played the introduction to the song while the band accompanied him. To hear Dinah Washington's song with real live instruments was just like the way I pictured it would sound. It was perfect and better than the actual record. Nothing sounded like *live* music.

Major gave Ali the okay symbol with his right hand before he said into the microphone, "Show a hand for the lady. She's singing the blues tonight."

As the crowd applauded, I rose to my shaking feet with a small smile on my face, and made my way to the stage. I kept my steps real close together, so my balance wouldn't go astray, took the microphone from Major's stand, and stood at the piano. I kept my eyes on him 'cause I was too afraid to walk center stage. I waited for some sort of cue. Since he assumed I knew when to start, he never did give me a cue and I had no idea when to begin the song.

Lord, please help me.

I felt like crying and would've jumped at the chance to hide underneath a rock or inside a cave if one was nearby.

Major nodded his head again, this time with his eyes piercing through me, and for some reason that intense look on his face eased the panic attack that was trying to happen. With the help of Ali's voice in my psyche, I cleared my throat, shut my eyes, and in my mind I was back at home in my bathroom. Suddenly, everyone faded from the room and I finally heard the cue on the second loop. I sang.

"Heaven please send all to mankind
Understanding and peace of mind
But if it's not asking too much
Please send me someone to love
Someone to love…"

Keeping my eyes shut, a surge of adrenaline pumped through my veins. I took in air through my diaphragm while exhaling out articulate consonants and vowels through my amplified sounds effortlessly. Through my abdominal and lower pelvic muscles, I projected my voice in a way that felt as free as a soaring eagle. Singing on that stage felt just as pleasant as it did when I got lost in my world and hit notes I only hit while in my bathroom. When the song came to an end, I opened my eyes and the whole house had come to life on their feet, applauding my rendition of the song.

Major went into his own heat filled solo, jooking those keys with such a fiery passion that had the crowd howling and whistling. I eased off the stage quickly with a shy smile and rejoined my group.

Georgia squeezed me and shouted over the boisterous crowd, "Kae Taylor, I knew you had that fire inside of you, but *guuuuurrrrllll*, you gave me the chills."

"Oh God, I was so nervous. Look, I'm still shaking." I showed her just how badly my ice cold hands were trembling.

She grabbed my shaking hands firmly between hers. "I could tell you were nervous, but honey, you knocked our socks off."

Niyah Moore

"It was so strange hearing my own voice on that microphone... didn't sound like me, but it was fun."

"You sounded... *perfect.*" Georgia's dimpled grin was so wide, I was sure her cheeks were hurting from smiling so.

I looked over at Ali who wore the same look of amazement as everyone else in the room. He said into my ear, "Now, that's how you sing the blues."

As badly as I wanted him to kiss me at that moment, he didn't. Instead, he kept his arm around me while my heart was no longer beating in fear, but it was now beating with anxiety to get back on stage.

***

Ed and Georgia's fighting resumed once we exited Bop City. All they did was bicker. Ed wanted to have his way with her again in his car. The only way Georgia would go was if he promised to get her to my house before the break of dawn. As soon as they made up their minds and cursed a few obscenities at one another, I waved them goodbye and stood outside with Ali.

"I'll walk you home in a little bit," Ali said.

"Okay."

Major was taking a smoke break near the curb. He seemed like he was in a very deep thought as he puffed on that Camel cigarette.

"You were cold on that piano tonight, Major," Ali said, sliding him some skin.

"Nah, the star tonight was this young lady right here. What's your name again?" Major asked as he blew out a bulky cloud of smoke.

"Kae Taylor."

"How old are you Kae Taylor?"

"I'm seventeen, but I'll be eighteen in a few months."

MAJOR JAZZ

"Young… Your voice is so mature, yet sweet like sugar," Major admired. All of a sudden as if a light bulb went off in his head, he said, "I got it. We 'gon call you Candy Cane Taylor from now on."

"Candy Cane?" I asked with a giggle. It sounded a bit silly to me.

"Yes… Candy Cane Taylor," Major recertified with a big smile, boasting his shiny gold tooth. Those hazel eyes of his shimmered underneath the light of the moon and almost looked aquatic.

"I dig it," Ali said. "It has a certain ring to it."

Major gave me a nickname and it stuck with me. I had impressed the master. That night, I felt like I had just bought a mansion in the sky.

Kae Taylor

It was only a few days after my first time on stage and we were already working on songs at Major's pad, a room he was renting somewhere between Sutter and Bush Street. Everything was going just fine, but I had to do more sneaking around behind my unsuspecting parents' back. I was running out of excuses and wasn't sure how much longer I was going to be able to keep up with the charade. My worst nightmare was to get caught by Daddy and the punishment that would ensue immediately.

Ali, Major, and I collaborated on writing songs. That was the fun part. When the three of us put our passionate minds together, the result was something amazing. We kept at it for a week straight, composing beautiful, original ballads every day. Major thought it would be a great idea to record as soon as we could pay for studio time, but meanwhile, he wanted me to sing along side him on Saturday nights. He got us a gig at the Primalon Ballroom, a roller-skating rink during the week and a nightclub on the weekends.

"You think you'll be ready to do a show at the Primalon Ballroom this Saturday?"

I hesitated and then paused. How was I going to tell my parents that their underage daughter landed a gig singing in a nightclub? I couldn't muster up the courage to do so. "I'm ready… but…"

"You sound real good," Ali said before I could finish my sentence.

"Thank you, but that's not what I was going to say."

"What's wrong?" Ali asked.

"Are you worried you look too young? We have to do somethin' 'bout the way you look. You have to become Candy Cane Taylor, the foxy blues singer. We have to get you dolled up," Major said.

"I can wear one of my mama's wigs. I need some clothes, but…"

"Don't worry 'bout the clothes," Major replied. "I'll have you fixed up before the weekend is up."

"What am I going to tell my parents?" I blurted out finally.

There was an awkward silence for a split second. It was like the thought never crossed their minds to ask my parents' permission to perform.

"You want me to talk to them?" Ali asked, rubbing the back of his neck with uncertainty.

"Somebody needs to ask 'em. My parents party around here and if they catch me on stage, my daddy will have no sweat snatching my tail off that stage and skinnin' me alive."

Major blew cigarette smoke from his mouth. "I'll lay it on them."

"You will?"

He nodded. "What time they get home this evening?"

"Mama is usually always home and Daddy should be home no later than seven, but they do step out after nine at night."

He nodded again while pouring himself some gin. I had never seen anyone drink so early in the day. It

Niyah Moore

seemed like Major always had a glass of liquor and a cigarette in his hand, no matter the time of day.

I smiled at Ali and he looked relieved that he wouldn't have to ask my parents. Major could do the hard work. It had been only a week since he tried to ask my father to take me out and he was still too nervous to ask again. I wanted him to win my father's heart the way he had won mine, so I didn't want him to give up. He was going to have to muster up the courage sometime.

***

Major Ingram sat in my living room with a glass of mama's lemonade on ice. He looked quite relaxed with his hat resting on his lap, which was far from the feeling I had. Felt like butterflies having a grand 'ole time, playing inside my tummy. As I peered through the side rails from the top of the stairs, I could only see Major because my parents were seated on the other side of the living room.

My father's strong southern voice carried through the house, "What brings you to my place of residence, Mr. Ingram?"

"I'm a pianist looking for a singer."

"I heard you play plenty of times. You're very talented."

"Thank you, sir… Your daughter, Kae, she-"

"What 'bout my daughter?" My father spat defensively.

Oh no, I thought to myself as I prayed my daddy wouldn't drag him by his coattail and kick him out if he gave off the wrong impression.

Major was poised as he responded, "I'm here to ask for your permission to allow her to accompany my band once a week on Saturday nights at the Primalon Ballroom."

MAJOR JAZZ

"The skating rink?"

"Well, yes, but they clear the rink and put the stage up. She'll be paid six dollars a night."

Silence fell on the room. Major sipped coolly on his lemonade, ready to rebut my father if he had to.

"She's only seventeen..." That was my mother's voice. "She only has a few more weeks before she's done with high school."

"And she's going to nursing school straight after that," Daddy declared, sternly.

I rolled my eyes. He had his heart set on me going to nursing school. I didn't want to break his heart, but this was my life.

"She won't be hanging out with the band after hours. My friend Sallie will bring her home at a decent hour. She'll be paid to record in Los Angeles, as well, if this pan out the way I think it should."

"You want her to make a record in Los Angeles?" My father's ears seemed to stand at attention. Anything involving a potential money growing situation was always a way to get my daddy to listen.

"Yes, sir... I have a few guys in Los Angeles who have been interested in recording a record for some time. All I need is a singer."

I heard a lighter flicker. That was my daddy lighting his smoking pipe. After a few seconds, I heard him ask, "Have you heard her sing before?"

I hoped Major was an excellent liar. I held my breath as I anticipated his ready response.

"No, I haven't."

Whew, relief.

"You want her to sing for you right now? See, my daughter has a fear of singin' in front of people. I'm sure you can find other singers that'll be willin' to perform."

Major replied, "Sure, I'd love to hear her if she'll sing for me."

I had no idea my father even paid attention to my fear of getting on stage. He never mentioned it before. It was time to show my daddy the little scared girl was no longer afraid or shy.

"Kae?" My father called from his deep southern drawl.

"Yes." I tried to make it like I wasn't already sitting on the stairs listening.

"Come down here for a moment."

I walked down. "Yes sir?"

"This gentleman, Mr. Major Ingram, is a piano player. He's lookin' for a singer to sing with him. Would you mind singin' somethin' for him?"

"Right now?"

"Yes, right now."

With my head lifted high, I answered sweetly, "Okay." I cleared my throat and sang a Billie Holiday tune.

"I don't know why, but I'm feeling so sad... I long to try something I never had... Never had no kissin'... Oh, what I've been missin'... Lover man, oh, where can you be? The night is cold and I'm so alone... I'd give my soul just to call you my own... Got a moon above me... But no one to love me... Lover man, oh, where can you be?"

My daddy's face nearly went grey as his mouth was slightly agape and his smoking pipe was ready for his next puff, only he couldn't smoke it.

Mama rubbed my father's back gently. "What you thinkin' honey?"

MAJOR JAZZ

"I'm thinkin' Mr. Ingram got himself a singer," Daddy replied with a slight frown as if he couldn't believe his own words.

Major showed those handsome big teeth... gold tooth shining brightly in the corner. His wide hazel eyes were dazzling. He, too, really liked my newfound confidence.

"Yes!" I screamed, jumped up and down, and gave my daddy the biggest hug I could give him.

"Wait a minute. If I think *any* funny business is goin' on, you *won't* be singin' anymore."

"I promise, Daddy. No funny business."

"*And* I want you to continue with your studies."

"Yes, sir."

I smiled at Major and he said to my father, "You and Mrs. Taylor are more than welcome to come down to the club and hear us on Saturday nights. I'm sure she'll make you real proud."

I continued to jump up and down. I could tread light, then, knowing my father was fine with me singing.

***

The first dress rehearsal was at Major's apartment. One of his beautiful lady friends, Sallie Aquino, came in with a satin blue dress, long matching gloves, and heels straight from her family's cleaners on Fillmore. I had taken one of my mother's wigs from her closet and put it on. After I dressed, Sallie put on my makeup. She was so good at it that I hardly recognized myself.

Major walked around me with a very serious face. His slight frown made me afraid that he didn't like the way the dress fit. He shook his head slowly before looking at Ali. "She sho' 'nuf look like a fox, don't she?"

"She sure does…" Ali licked his lips and for the first time I saw his sexual desire for me. He couldn't take his eyes off me.

"Do I look old enough?" I asked, going back to a mirror to stare at myself.

"You pass," Major replied. "What you think, Sallie?"

"I think she looks absolutely stunning and not just because I dolled her either."

Who was I? I looked at myself in his slender mirror. I didn't have curvy hips like my mother, but I had a little something in the back. In that short, cropped wig, I looked like I belonged on someone's stage.

Major clapped his hands twice. "Well, all right now. I'm waiting for them damned Alley Cats to get here." He took a look at the clock on the wall.

Tyrone and Tyrell Alley, fraternal twins, were named amongst the top musicians in Fillmore. Tyrone beat those drums and Tyrell blew that sax as if it was their last night breathing.

"Candy Cane, show me how you're gonna stand and hold that microphone." Major brought the microphone stand to me.

I grabbed the microphone with my gloved hand, timidly, to take it off the stand. "Like this…"

"No, no, no, no…" Major shook his head vigorously. "I want you to gently take the microphone in your right hand and hold it up to your lips like this." He demonstrated a sensual pose while still looking very masculine.

I giggled as he handed it back to me. Imitating the same pose, I nearly kissed the microphone.

"Yes, just like that. Now, look at yourself in the mirror and practice singing while holding it just like that. Even if you rest it on the stand, grasp it and give me sex appeal."

I giggled again, dropping my eyes bashfully. "I'm not sure if I can…"

He was expecting me to do something that made me feel uncomfortable. I hadn't flirted with a man, so I knew nothing about being sexy.

Major bellowed roughly, "You are no longer Kae Taylor on that stage!"

I swallowed, but my throat felt so tight I didn't think my saliva could manage to slide down. I looked over at Ali to see what he thought of what Major was trying to make me do. His eyes told me he wanted to see if I had it in me.

Grabbing the microphone, I pretended like I was looking at Ali. Though Ali hadn't asked me out on any more dates, I dreamed he did. Music business was the only thing he seemed most concerned with and that made me wonder if music was the only thing he was really interested in from the start. Doubt had me, but hope filled me. One day, he would be mine.

I practiced holding the microphone and singing until Tyrone and Tyrell arrived. Before they set up, they went ahead and introduced themselves.

"Hello, my name is Tyrone Alley." He was a little taller than his twin brother with a slight gap between his teeth.

"Nice to meet you, Tyrone," I said, extending my hand to shake it, but he kissed the top of it instead. I blushed.

"And I'm Tyrell, the good-lookin' twin."

He was slightly darker than Tyrone and he was the better looking twin, and married. His wedding band told me that.

"Hello, Tyrell. It's such a pleasure to finally meet the infamous Alley Twins."

"You mean Alley Cats," Major corrected. "They some damned street Negroes."

They laughed.

"It's a good thing I ain't short tempered or…" Tyrone said.

"Oh, I flies hot quick," Tyrell interrupted his brother, "so, Major better watch it."

Major retorted, "You mighty easy cooled if the man is bigger than you."

They all erupted into a hearty laughter.

Tyrone sat at the drum set. He hit the hi-hat a few times and his foot smashed the pedal. Tyrell took out his sax from his bag and adjusted the reed. I stood in front of the mic, ready to sing when they were ready.

Major gave them the sheet music. "We ready?" he asked, growing impatient with how long it was taking them to get ready. That man had the worst patience in the world.

The twins nodded.

"From the top!" Major shouted, sitting at the piano. He played the introduction to the ballad.

The Alley Cats joined in, I sang on cue, and we practiced both songs that late Friday afternoon until the sun went down. Major was a perfectionist and took his music very seriously. If I hit one note that was off key, he would stop the music and demand to start all over again.

"Hold it, hold it, hold it… Now, Kae, you have to hit that note! I need you to SANG!"

When we were finally done, I removed the clothes, wig, and makeup in the tiny bathroom down the hall.

Sallie wrapped the dress in plastic as soon as I came out. "I'll meet you at the Ballroom tomorrow night.

MAJOR JAZZ

Major wants me to take the dress down to my family's cleaners for a clean and press."

"Okay. Thank you for everything, Sallie."

"You're welcome, honey. By the way, you sounded good."

"Thank you. See you later."

She smiled.

I went down the hall into Major's apartment and waved. "Good night everyone, I'll see you tomorrow night."

"Good night," they said in unison.

"Are you walking home alone?" Ali asked with a slight frown. He looked at the time on his watch.

"Yes, unless you want to walk me..."

"Well, I wouldn't want you to go walking around this neighborhood at this time of night." He said to the band, "Good night everyone."

They all said good night. Ali opened the door for me and we left out of the apartment.

"You looked real pretty in that dress tonight."

"Do you think it's too much? I mean, Major is going overboard with this foxy act, don't you think? I just want to sing."

He shook his head and scratched his temple. "It's a little risky, but it's only to be age appropriate. I trust Major knows just what he's doing and you should, too." He was hesitant before he uttered, "I'm not going to lie, you... um... made me kind of excited... if you know what I mean…"

I laughed because I knew exactly what he meant. I was curious to find out more. "Do you ever think of me that way?"

"Yeah I do, but I respect you. You're a good girl."

"Thank you. You're a good man."

"I'm no saint. I've been around a block or two if you know what I mean. I know you don't have any experience with dating, so I've been waiting for the right time to make my move... I really want to be your boyfriend someday."

I stopped walking and stared at him to make sure he wasn't pulling my leg. "You want to go steady someday?"

He stopped alongside me. "I want to do that and more... sooner than later... But, it's no rush. Whenever you're ready."

Chills covered my entire body as if an unexpected breeze drifted across me.

"I think you're sweet," was all I could say.

"I try to be."

Since he was leaving this up to me, I said, "I'm ready."

"So, you'll go steady with me?"

I couldn't stop the grin from covering my face. "Yes."

"Would you mind if I kissed you right now?" I could see him swallow hard. He was afraid I would protest, but I didn't.

Before I could answer his question, he placed his hands around the small of my back to draw me close to him. His heavenly scent greeted me and I inhaled him with my eyes closed tightly. He lowered his lips to touch mine and they were so soft... felt like two tiny pillows. I was glad I waited to have my first kiss from him. He had been worth the wait.

My hands never left my side. That's how scared I was. When I opened my eyes to look up at him, I realized I wasn't dreaming. He had really kissed me. He backed away gently before he could get too carried away while taking my hand into his. We walked the rest of the way to my house, hand in hand, in complete silence. He seemed to be lost for words, himself.

All the lights in my house were off. That meant my parents were out having a good time. Suddenly, a wild thought came to mind. "You want to come in?" I don't know where it came from. I just knew that I wasn't ready for him to leave, plus the sensation between my legs wanted to find out how he was making me tingle so.

He smiled while looking away from me. Then, his eyes scanned mine as if he were in deep thought before he politely declined, "No, I think I should go on home. Plus, I don't think your parents would like that too much."

"Can I come with you then? My parents won't be back 'til later. It's only nine o'clock. They're just getting down to the Texas Playhouse."

He looked a little uneasy as his eyes looked at my dark house. "I don't think that would be such a good idea either. I don't want you to be uncomfortable and I for sure don't want Mr. Taylor to worry."

"I'm not uncomfortable and he's not coming home for a few more hours. I really don't want you to leave me right now. How far do you live?"

"Just a few blocks from here."

I slipped my hand back into his, knowing what could possibly happen once at his place and that's exactly what I wanted to experience. With only three months until my eighteenth birthday, I felt I was grown enough to handle whatever was to happen that night. I was more than ready to prove that to him.

"Do you think your grandmother would mind if I visited for a little while?"

"Not at all… She's probably sleeping or on her way to sleep anyway."

Niyah Moore

"Do you bring many women into your house?"

He frowned a little, but answered honestly, "I've had a few women, but only had one love and that's the only love I've ever had. She moved away with her family last year. Since she's been gone, I've been too focused on school and writing, but then, I met you..."

Once again, that feeling of floating amongst the moon was upon me. With my small hand resting in his big hand, we walked.

***

We quietly entered the dimly lit Victorian home. His grandmother was fast asleep in her bedroom and didn't hear a thing.

"Would you like anything to drink?" he asked.

"No, I'm fine."

Down at the very end of the hallway was his bedroom. As soon as he closed the door, my heart started pounding, but not in a frightened way... more of an anxious way. I wanted to know what it felt like to be kissed all over with his soft lips.

I stood in the middle of his tidy bedroom, unsure of what to do next. He went to the window and opened it so the bay air could sweep in. It was a bit chilly that summer's night, but I didn't mind the breeze because my body temperature was climbing quickly and I needed all the air I could get. Suddenly, I felt bold enough to invade his personal space. I planted my feet right in front of his, wrapped my arms around his neck, and tilted my head back so I could stare into his eyes.

I loved those eyes.

He tried to make conversation to divert the sexual tension. "Rehearsal went well, don't you think? The band is really making that song out nice. I feel it in my bones. I-"

MAJOR JAZZ

I subdued his words with a long kiss. The heated passion emerged from inside of me as if it were trapped in a sealed vessel and slowly released. He wrapped his strong arms around me tightly as if he never wanted to let go.

His sensual kisses on my mouth, chin, and neck had me feeling more than ready to give myself to him. We lay on his squeaky bed. It was finally happening. I was living out a real life love scene. Once he started removing my clothing, I realized what I had gotten myself into. Was I really ready to be had? A part of me panicked when I thought of how painful it would be. Georgia told me many stories of how badly it hurt when she lost her virginity. I clenched the side of the bed and closed my eyes as tight as I could.

"I want you to concentrate on the way I make you feel. Don't think about anything else. I'll be extremely gentle. Let my passion consume you."

His smooth hands were between my thighs, rubbing that tingly throbbing spot through my panties. As my shirt came unbuttoned, he kissed my shoulders. Removing my bra, he kissed between my breasts, and licked my nipples, teasing them with his tongue. My skirt was next as he licked along my thighs and down to my ankles.

My breathing had become so heavy; all I could hear was me. I grew more aroused each and every time his lips touched any part of my flesh. Soon, we were both completely naked, kissing while in each other's arms and taking our time in the moment. I really didn't know what to do with my hands, but I kept them busy by roaming his back, chest, and arms. Felt right and he didn't seem to care as long as they were on his body.

As I rode his waves of love, I was no longer in his bedroom, but surrounded by a beach landscape and dancing along his oceanic shore. Our breathing, our oxygen, shared and matched the same tempo as we exhaled passion into one other's mouths—suffocating my fear with heavy air of adoration.

That night, I let him have me.

That night, we became lovers.

That night, I was no longer a virgin.

That night, I became a woman.

Kae Taylor

On Saturday afternoons, my mother always cooked pancakes, bacon, and eggs as if it were still morning. Whenever my parents had a long night out, she cooked breakfast at lunchtime. Her pancakes always came out so fluffy, never burnt, and picture perfect golden brown just like the picture on the Bisquick box. Drenched in butter and syrup, they melted in my mouth. The smell of her cooking made my stomach rumble and helped me to get out of bed to brush my teeth. Daddy was drinking coffee by the time I made my way downstairs and I kissed him on the cheek.

"Good afternoon. Do you want some brunch?" Mama flipped a flapjack.

"Yes, ma'am. I'm starving." I tried to talk normally, but a raspy whisper came out instead. My vocal chords had been worn out during all the singing at rehearsal.

I plopped down at the table and felt throbbing from the swollen soreness between my legs. I thought a long bath would help, but it didn't do much. I couldn't wrap my mind around how gentle Ali was during our love making, yet I ached between my thighs like I had been in a twelve round bout with the heavy weight champion of the world.

"Oh, you don't sound too good." Mama frowned. "You want some hot tea to soothe that throat? You have to sing tonight."

"Yes, please."

"What time you get in last night?" Daddy looked up from his newspaper with one eyebrow slightly raised. That stern expression always made him look a little evil.

"We wrapped up rehearsal around seven thirty and I got home around eight."

He took a good look at me while I reached over to grab the freshly squeezed orange juice from the glass carafe sitting in the middle of the table.

"We called to make sure everything was alright. You didn't answer," Daddy said.

"I didn't hear the phone. Rehearsal really had me beat."

Still, his eyes pierced me.

I drank some juice.

"What's this nonsense I hear 'bout you dating Ali Watson... behind my back?"

My eyes widened. Instantly, I thought of denying it, but I was too stunned to respond. I lowered my guilty eyes and didn't put up a fight. I'm sure the tears that started to well up confirmed the truth.

"Answer me. Haven't you?" he barked out, suddenly.

I was startled by how loud he spoke, but honest words still refused to come out.

"He's a good boy, Earl," Mama stated while pouring water into the kettle. "He goes to college. He's studying journalism and writes poetry. His grandmother eats at our place all the time. You know, Erma Jean? That's his grandmother. She raised him and brags all the time about how proud of him she is."

Niyah Moore

My father grunted, keeping his eyes on me. "She's too young to date. Bad enough I'm letting her pursue this singin' mess, but only 'cause I know she's so passionate 'bout it."

"She's no younger than we were when you asked my father to court me. You 'member how nervous you were to even ask him?"

"Hmmm, yeah... Twenty-three years ago... I was nervous, but I waited for his approval. I didn't go 'round sneakin' behind his back. I waited to have you 'til we were married."

Shame loomed over me. We hadn't waited until we were married to be intimate, even though I didn't do anything I didn't want to do that night. Ali was the perfect gentleman and I had a great time, so I didn't understand why I was feeling so bad.

"I'm sure Ali Watson is gonna wait too, right Kae?"

"Yes ma'am," I replied quickly.

"See, Earl. Give the girl a break. At least he's not one of these hoodlums out here on these corners. I like him."

"You like him, huh?" He grunted again.

"Yes, I like him. He's in college."

"Well, I don't see what you like 'bout him. Just 'cause he a college boy, what that mean? College boys break hearts too."

"I agree, but Kae is almost eighteen years old and someone is going to break her heart one day. We all go through it. When you think is appropriate for her to have a boyfriend?"

"It's not appropriate any time."

"Now, Earl..."

"She can do whatever she wants after she finishes the nursing program."

MAJOR JAZZ

Mama put the kettle on the burner and placed her hand on her wide hip. "Now, Earl Taylor, that don't make no sense. You expect her to be an old maid then?"

"You god-damned skippy." That was my daddy's saying whenever he was adamant about something.

"Ali is a good boy. I can tell it. I don't want Kae sneaking off behind our backs. What you think she gonna do anyway?"

Huffing and puffing for a few seconds, he rubbed his round belly and uttered, "Well... I guess it's alright. As long as he picks you up from here when I'm home and return you at a decent hour... Ya hear me?"

I smiled a little... didn't want to seem too excited, but I was more than happy about his approval. "Thank you so much, Daddy."

"No more talkin', Kae. You have to rest your voice. I want you to drink this tea, suck on this here lemon, and wrap a heated towel around your throat. Looks like I'm goin' to the club with you to make sure you are properly seen afta."

"While y'all do that, I'll be down at the restaurant takin' care of some things."

Once he went to work, he always got swamped. "Daddy..."

"Don't fret. I'll be at the Ballroom just in time for your performance."

Mama made Daddy's plate first, and then mine. Once she fixed hers, we all ate together without speaking. Daddy was into his newspaper and then left to go to work as soon as he had chomped his meal down. As soon as the kettle whistled, Mama poured tea into two china cups with lemon and honey and then sat back down next to me.

When my eyes met hers, she narrowed her eyes, and shook her head with a sly smile. "How long you thank you can hide your secret from me?"

"Huh?"

"Don't you huh me, heifer... I'm your mother and I notice things you think I can't. You even walked into this kitchen differently. Your daddy might not notice somethin' like that, but I'm a woman, honey. Look at me... You weren't home last night. You let him get your cherry pie last night, didn't you?"

I hadn't known my mother to be so vulgar, but I never could hide too much from her. She allowed me to be able to share things on my mind, in secret, just between us two, and this was one of those sacred moments.

With tears threatening to pour from my eyes, I replied assertively, "It was my idea to go to his place. He didn't pressure me and I felt it was time to become a woman."

"Hmmm, I remember those days like it was yesterday. We only waited 'til marriage 'cause Earl was terrified of my daddy's rifle..." She laughed at the memory. "Now, you ain't gonna get pregnant, are you?"

"No, ma'am."

"I know you want to be grown up and I like him, but please don't get pregnant. It will break your daddy's heart."

"Okay."

"Did Ali tell you I had a talk with him the other day?"

My eyes grew wide. I shook my head without speaking.

"He was at the cleaners talkin' to the man behind the counter 'bout his new venture, writin' songs for you and Major and thangs… I turned to him and introduced myself as Lola Taylor, your mother, and the way he looked at me when he talked 'bout you, I knew he had been bitten by the love bug." She chuckled. "I trust that you're old enough to make the right decisions. This is your first time being in love. Just promise me you don't end up pregnant before you're married. That's my only request."

"I promise… Can I ask you a question?"

"Sure."

"What do I do about this sore feeling?"

Mama laughed at me so hard, she put both of her hands on her cheeks and shook her head. "Now, you gonna to have to duke it out, but it should subside by the morning 'less you do it again before then."

I pouted to myself. I didn't think the after effect of sex would hurt so badly.

She kissed me on the forehead and finished up the dishes. "Now, rest that pretty lil' voice of yours. I'm so jazzed about this show tonight. I done called all my friends."

***

I took another bath and rested my voice for the remainder of the day, drinking nothing but soothing, hot tea. As it got later, Mama nearly worried me to death over leaving to get to the Ballroom on time. Major called before we left and gave specific instructions on what to do once in the dressing room. I had to warm up my voice while Sallie did my makeup and got me dressed.

My mama couldn't believe her eyes after she saw me in my makeup and dress. "Is that my wig?" she asked with a hard frown.

I nodded slowly, afraid she would snatch it off. "Does it look weird?"

Niyah Moore

"No, you look absolutely beautiful," she said with tears welling up into her eyes. "Sallie, you have my baby lookin' so grown."

"Mama, please don't cry."

It was too late. She was reaching for tissue. "I'm not." She turned away quickly to hide her face from me. "Wait, 'til your father sees you. He's not gonna believe it."

As Sallie touched up my makeup, I admired her Asian looking eyes and pretty, dark hair that looked like China silk. I wondered what her parents looked like as she said, "Showtime is in fifteen minutes. Are you nervous?"

"No, I'm ready."

There was a knock on the door.

Sallie said, "Come in."

Ali entered. He looked handsome, as always, in his suit. It was our first time seeing one another since we bonded and butterflies danced at the sight of him.

"Good evening, Mrs. Taylor," he said to my mother with a brief hug and kiss on her cheek. "Mr. Taylor is in the audience, front row, and your seat is right next to his."

"Thank you... I'm goin' to my seat now."

I felt relieved that she was finally getting out of the dressing room. She was driving me crazy. "Okay Mommy. Wish me luck."

"Good luck."

As soon as she was out of the room, I exhaled. "That woman makes me so nervous."

Ali grinned before he placed a kiss on my cheek. "I would kiss those lips I love so much, but I don't want to ruin your face dressing."

"Thank you for being careful," Sallie said. "I would hate to have to retouch before goin' on stage."

She went to the other side of the dressing room to give us some space to ourselves.

"How'd you sleep?" I asked.

"Like a baby, thanks to you. How are you feeling?"

"I feel good..."

He embraced me. "You look beautiful as always."

"Thank you."

"I really want to spend some time with you tomorrow afternoon."

My heart skipped to a happy beat. "Did you ask my father?"

"Yes, I got that covered already."

"You sure you got the okay this time?"

"Yes and everything is a go... Where's Georgia?"

"She's at home. She doesn't want my parents to see her sneaking out of the house."

"Gotcha…"

Major opened the door roughly and yelled inside, "Showtime! Let's go!"

I squeezed Ali and he placed a light kiss in the crook of my neck. He whispered against my skin, "I love you."

I didn't hesitate to reply, "I love you, too."

***

The large ballroom was packed and the three original songs we performed received a standing ovation. The rush of being in front of an audience left me feeling like I was flying and I didn't have to close my eyes. I was nearly out of breath at the end of the last song, but that was fine with me. The way the crowd clapped, I felt as if I never wanted to get off stage.

Major played another song, an instrumental featuring trumpet player, Frank Blue. Frank was the deepest, darkest black man I had ever seen, yet ruggedly handsome. I had never met Frank before that night; I only knew great things about him and that horn he blew.

Once I heard the sound come out of Frank's horn during his solo, I felt his soul. Frank Blue had me mesmerized. It was like whatever pain he felt from this world was much deeper and more profound than any other common source of pain to produce a beautiful sound.

"Wooooooow," I said to myself. "Outta sight...."

Ali joined me backstage and showered me with kisses. "Now, I finally get to kiss off that lip stain," he teased before giving me a kiss.

I giggled in his arms. Our kisses had evolved quite a bit. The cute little pecks were saved for when we were around other people. "Too bad I can't leave with you tonight."

"Why can't you? Your parents are going to Major's house party after this."

"But now that they know you and I are seeing one another, they'll probably be home a lot sooner," I said.

"Maybe or maybe not... Maybe they'll let me take you to dinner."

"Maybe..."

We giggled at our "maybes".

I kissed him again before we went into the dressing room.

A knock on the dressing room door interrupted us before we could get into another lip locking session. "Come in," Ali said.

MAJOR JAZZ

A middle-aged Caucasian man with neatly combed hair entered. "Candy Cane Taylor?"

"Yes…" My eyebrows were raised.

"You were remarkable tonight. My name is Bob Schwartz. I'm from Los Angeles and I'm in the record business. Do you have a manager?"

I frowned a little. I knew nothing about the executive side of the music industry back then. I just loved to sing. Before I could reply, Ali answered, "Yes, she does. I'm her manager, Ali Watson. How can I help you?"

"I work for Terrace Records and we want to cut a record with Candy in Los Angeles. Major Ingram is a very good friend of mine and he marveled at how wonderful you are. I came down here to see for myself and was blown away. Your voice is amazing. It has so much depth to it."

"You want to sign her to a deal or what is it exactly that you want?"

"We want to record one single record with Candy and see how well that goes… see how the audience perceives her. Then, if things go well, she'll have herself a record deal."

"Oh, my God," I shrieked, grabbing Ali's arm tight.

Ali, on the other hand, remained cool. "I'm sure that'll be fine. We just have to clear a few things in our schedules. When do you want her out that way?"

"Well, as soon as possible."

"Will the weekend do?"

Ali was keeping in mind that I had school. School was almost over and very close to graduation day. I didn't need to miss a single day.

"Here, take my card. Give me a call when you can make it. Just don't keep me waiting too long." Bob

Niyah Moore

smiled, shook our hands, and left out of the dressing room.

"Baby, I'm gonna be on a record!"

"I'm proud of you. Major did hint that someone would be here tonight."

"This is amazing."

"Now, I just have to study on the music business. I know nothing about being a manager."

I squeezed him. "I like how you're so quick on your feet. You're going to be the best manager ever."

"And your dream is coming true."

***

Ali and I rode with Major and Sallie seven and half hours to Los Angeles from San Francisco in his convertible top Chevy Bel Air. See, around that time, Major was making good money with all the gigs he had landed. I watched Sallie play in his wavy hair while he drove. The whole time I kept wondering how come Major messed around on her. Although, Sallie seemed to be the one he saw most often. I couldn't figure out their love thing. It wasn't any of my business, so I kept my questions and comments to myself.

We were in Hollywood and I was in a studio getting ready to sing my very first record. It was strange how I wasn't nervous to get on stage any more, but being in a room with a microphone and a band had me feeling nauseated. I threw up twice before I could get into the studio. My nerves were real bad.

"You okay?" Ali asked concerned while embracing me in the hallway.

"I'm so nervous… I just had to get it out."

"Here's some water. They're ready for you when you are. Take your time."

MAJOR JAZZ

I drank cool water from a paper cup. "Okay, I'll be ready in a few more minutes."

"You look terrified."

"I am…"

"Hey, the good thing about recording is that if it doesn't come out right, they can just stop and do it again until its right. You can stop as many times as you need to."

"Is that how this works?"

He kissed my forehead. "You're going to do just fine. Major is going over the song with the songwriter, Diane. She has written a beautiful ballad. It's not like the blues you're used to singing."

"What you think about it?"

"I like it. It's real catchy."

After a few more minutes of drinking water, I went into the studio to learn the song the talented Diane had written. She sang it to me while Major and the rest of the band played. It was such a fresh sound, a Rhythm and Blues track. It sure sounded like a hit record to me.

It didn't take long to learn it because I always learned songs fast. She told me to put my own sound to it. Once I heard the track playback, I couldn't believe how beautiful I sounded. That was really me coming through the speakers and I felt so proud.

"We love it. We can't wait to get it into rotation on the radio," Bob said to Major.

Major looked like he was meditating with closed eyes while listening to the song. He was such a passionate musician, one who could hear every little riff, and he had a good ear to make the decisions to make the song perfect. He didn't complain or add any input that time. That meant he loved it, too.

We spent a few hours in the studio recording the song and it didn't require a whole lot of takes. We were able to leave before the sun went down.

"Are we heading back tonight?" Ali asked Major. "It's kind of late."

"Yeah, I don't want to stay out here too long. It's not safe like it is in Fillmore... too much racism." Major's voice trailed off as if he didn't want to relive his bad experiences.

I knew racism existed, but we didn't experience it much in San Francisco, except if we wanted to do certain things downtown. That was the reason why we did everything in Fillmore. There was no need to go anywhere else.

Kae Taylor

With a hit record on the airwaves, I had become a local celebrity in my neighborhood. My record was playing on bay area radio KROW 960AM. Bob at Terrace Records was doing his best to get it played wherever he could. A contract was possibly in the works if we were successful. Everyone who heard the record loved it just as much as we did. While I was enjoying my local success, graduation was a week away and I was ready to finish so I could start doing shows on the road. I wasn't sure if I was going to be the next big thing, but it felt good just to walk the streets and be acknowledged as a star.

In the meantime, I continued to be a teenager in love. I still studied for finals, Ali and I had become even closer, and I spent every moment I could with him. One of his favorite things to do was to read his poems to me from his grandmother's porch.

Lay before me
Give me your unsettled worries
I will obliterate them
*   to an irrelevant indistinct place*
They may pile up on me
But, I don't mind
Your reserve tank may fill with heartbreak
I shall gather them into galleries of silence
Garnish my shoulders with your cares

So that you can intoxicate me
Fill me with your passion-filled scent
So that your love may dance in my heart forever

As I listened, I couldn't help but feel like I was the luckiest girl on the planet. The way he showed his affection through his words was something that left me feeling high as if I were floating amongst the clouds and residing there.

"What you think about that one?"

"I love you."

"I love you, too. Lately, all my poems have been about love."

"I noticed… Whoever she is, you must really love her."

Embracing me in his arms, he replied with his eyebrows burrowed deep into his forehead, "I'm looking at her. I'm crazy about you."

I laughed into his chest and then replied, "I'm even crazier about you."

"Is that so?"

"That is so."

He stopped squeezing me so tight so that I could breathe. "What do you have planned for the rest of the day?"

"I'm goin' to hang with Georgia. I haven't seen her in a while."

"Alright, I have some studying to do for finals. I hope I get that intern job at the paper."

"There is no doubt in my mind. I know you'll get it. I'll see you later at rehearsal."

"Ah, I can't make rehearsal tonight. I have to study."

"Oh," I whined. "I'll be home after rehearsal, so call me to say good night."

"I will."

Niyah Moore

He kissed me goodbye and I walked home with nothing on my mind but my happiness and how truly good life had been to me. I couldn't complain. Everything in my world felt too perfect up until I saw Georgia sitting on the steps of her porch, legs up to her chest, and her head buried in her arms.

As I crossed over to her lawn, I said, "Hey Georgia... I'm getting ready to come on over, but I have to go to the bathroom first." I noticed she was wiping her tears.

She looked up at me with her face soaked. "I'm fine.... Or at least I'm gonna be."

I didn't hesitate to sit next to her. "I haven't seen you cry since we were little. What's wrong?"

"I'm pregnant..." she gasped for air as fresh tears streaked her face, "and Ed doesn't want to be a daddy..."

"What you mean he don't want to be a daddy? He doesn't have a choice."

"He broke up with me."

"What?"

"Yes, Ed broke up with me." More tears fell as she cried.

"Aw, Georgia, he'll be back. He always comes back."

"I believe him this time.... He's done with me. I know it. He doesn't want anything to do with me."

"Aw, he's just talkin' foolish. He doesn't mean that."

"I think he does. God, I'm so afraid to tell my parents. How am I gonna tell 'em?"

"I guess you have to find some way to let them know... Well, at least we graduate next week."

More tears poured as she stared out at the street, shaking her head. "I know it, without a doubt, my life is

MAJOR JAZZ

officially ruined. I tried to talk to Ed's mother and she thinks I got pregnant on purpose to get Ed to marry me. She hates me."

"She'll come around. She has to. You're about to have her grandchild. You just have to give them some time. Everything will be okay. I know it."

"No! Everything won't be okay!" Georgia stood up with her fists balled up tightly. "What do you know anyway? You think you're better than me, don't you? With your fancy new clothes and fancy recording deal! You don't know nothin' 'bout what I'm goin' through."

I scowled, standing to my feet as well, defensively. "What are you talking about? I'm only trying to console you."

"I haven't seen you 'round here... It's like you forgot all 'bout me. You don't need me anymore. You and Ali do everything that we used to do together. Maybe you should just leave me alone for good."

"Georgia, I'm only gonna let you talk crazy to me 'cause I know you are going through some things and you don't understand what's going on."

"Leave me alone! Take your happy ass off my porch. Go live your happy, perfect life!" She stormed up the steps and slammed her front door.

My chest started heaving and tears poured down my face. Her words had truly hurt me. My best friend no longer wanted to be my best friend and I didn't really understand why. I wasn't sure why she said what she said that day, but I realized she was missing the time we used to spend together. With tears blurring my vision, I went home and cried.

***

Everyone my parents knew came to our house to wish me luck on my future endeavors, except for Georgia, and for that I was heartbroken. She didn't

even go to the graduation ceremony amongst our schoolmates. I left my own party distraught, went into my bedroom, and cried tears that seemed to be endless.

Mama knocked on my door before she came in. "Honey, what's wrong?"

I cried, "Georgia's mad at me and there's nothing I can do to fix it. I've tried everything. She won't even look at me."

"What she got to be mad 'bout?"

"She thinks I abandoned our friendship because of Ali and now she's about to have a baby. I feel like a horrible friend."

She shook her head. "That's a shame. It's a big responsibility takin' care of a baby. Sometimes, when you grow up, you also grow out of friends. I lost my best friend when I moved here from Texas." She held me to her breasts and gently rubbed the top of my head. "In this thing we call life, shit happens... I'm sorry it hurts you like this. You'll be just fine in time. Clean your face, chile."

"Okay," I sniffled.

"Ali said he has an announcement to make and he wants everyone in the front room, so I need you to look real pretty. No one can be happy with you if you're not happy. You have family and other friends who want to celebrate with you. So, get on down here." She left out.

I dried my tears and pulled myself together before rejoining my party.

Ali put his arm around me when I stood next to him. "Mr. Taylor gave me permission to ask the woman I love for her hand in marriage..."

My dad raised his glass of scotch and soda.

He got down on one knee in front of me while I stood there with my mouth wide open. "Will you marry me, Kae Taylor?"

MAJOR JAZZ

Without a thought, question, or anything, I blurted out, "Yes, I'll marry you!"

He slid the ring onto my finger as our guests congratulated us. A fairytale was what I felt I was living. I cried again, but not sad tears, tears of joy.

***

"What happened to Kae's money?" I overheard Major on the phone with Terrace Records.

Though he was trying to be discreet about the phone call in his kitchen, I could hear him from his living room. I mean his apartment was so small, you could see the entire place from where I was standing. I felt something wasn't quite right. After a few more uh huhs and alrights, he was off of the phone, looking like he was sick to his stomach. Major's hazel eyes were filled with so much worry that the pit of my own stomach churned.

"Kae..." He poured a glass a gin. "Terrace isn't interested in signing you. They feel you're too young and need some more experience."

"But, the record is doing so well. I thought-"

"Locally, but they can't get anyone to spin it anywhere else. All we can do is to keep trying."

"What about the money they owe me for the song?"

"They said that was to pay for studio time... I'm really sorry. We'll deal with someone else. We don't need them."

I was disappointed, but I didn't let that get me down. On the positive side, I was still singing at the Ballroom and that was suiting me just fine.

"I wrote a new song," I said to ease up the mood. "I want to try it out sometime soon."

Niyah Moore

He drank his gin and lit a cigarette. "We can try it out next week. I'm a bit tired tonight."

Major wasn't tired because he was never too tired to play music. He was let down. He didn't want to make it seem as if he had broken a promise. A dark cloud hovered over him like a warning sign of a thunderstorm and though I didn't know much about him other than sounds, I could tell just how bad he felt.

"Are we still rehearsing tonight? Where's everyone else?"

"No, I cancelled rehearsal earlier. I meant to tell you. We're gonna do somethin' we know Saturday."

"Okay." I grabbed my coat from his couch to leave.

"Congratulations again on your proposal. Ali is a good man. I've known him since we were kids. He's gonna take care of you for the rest of your life and you'll have pretty babies." He smiled and tilted his glass towards me.

"Thank you. Most women want to do nothing but be a wife and mother, but I dream of being so much more than that. I'll be enrolling in music school soon."

"If singing is what you want to do, follow your heart and never let your dreams escape you."

"I won't… What's your plans, Major? What is it that you dream of?"

"I don't dream. I just do what I want to do. I love the 'Mo. My heart and soul is right here. If I don't ever make it big in music at least I have my piano. As long as I have my music I'm happy." Through his eyes, I could see sadness, though his words were happy. There was something inside of him that pained him. I was sure it was too deep for me to understand at that age.

MAJOR JAZZ

"Fillmore isn't going anywhere. The world needs to see and hear you. If you went to New York, you would definitely make it."

"I know I would do well in the Big Apple... I just feel like I'm gonna miss out on somethin' so great here."

"You can always come back," I said.

"True." He poured more gin.

"Are we still having rehearsal tomorrow?"

"Yeah, I'll see you tomorrow."

"I'll see you tomorrow."

I continued to sing in Fillmore for a few more years, but I never got that record deal I dreamed of. Things just didn't work out that way for me. I married Ali and we bought a house in Oakland when the Fillmore Housing Redevelopment came and pushed everyone out. We raised two children... boys. I became a reputable vocal coach. Ali went on to become Senior Editor at the Chronicle and published a book of his poetry. Our boys grew up, went to college, got married, and gave us grandsons. Those grandsons gave us a host of great-granddaughters. Our love didn't waiver, not once during sixty-five years of marriage.

By the end of 1965, the Fillmore was completely gone. People started calling the redevelopment the Negro Removal of San Francisco, and the horrible press kept saying it was only done because the housing in the Fillmore was falling apart and had become too crowded. There was too much crime and too many minorities. They talked about our neighborhood like it was some ghetto slum. It was nowhere near a *ghetto* or a *slum* to us. Fillmore was the best place I ever lived, still to this day, but there was nothing anyone could do to save it. No matter how many meetings were set up and no matter how much we protested, over a fifteen year span, the Fillmore we knew and loved so much was gone. It's still so sad. I remember the bulldozers and how they destroyed it all. They handed out vouchers of a promise to return, and for most, the opportunity just never came.

Frank's Blues

*B*AM! BAM! BAM! BAM! BAM!
A series of hard knocks on my front door startled me right when I was trying to collar a nod and get some sleep. At first, I lay there hoping whoever was on the other side of the door would go away because I wasn't expecting company and didn't want to be bothered, but the knocks wouldn't let up and only got louder.

BAM! BAM! BAM! BAM! BAM!

I made myself get off the couch to answer it, though it was strenuous to do so. For some odd reason I was confused because I thought I was in my king sized bed, but I clearly didn't make it there. I must've passed out while listening to some records. My body felt as if it weighed a ton with every step I took and every time I blinked it felt like sand was in my eyes.

"Who is it?" I bellowed while scratching my itchy arms.

"Open up… It's me… Major."

I fumbled with the locks before I finally got it open.

Major walked in and glared at me. "Nice to see you're still alive."

"Hey, what's cookin'?" I avoided his stare, couldn't look him in the eyes. My guilty conscious wouldn't let me. I knew what I had done and knew why he came looking for me. "What time is it?"

"Frank, it's eleven-somethin'."

"In the mornin'?"

Major went over to the window and drew back the curtain to let in the unwanted sun. "Yes in the mornin'. Say, what in the hell happened to you last night? I waited for you and called, but the line was dead." He noticed the telephone was off the hook, so he put it back in the cradle. "I'm sure I would've been able to reach you if this wasn't off the hook... Why'd you miss the recording session?"

I flopped down on the couch, feeling as if I wanted him to get lost so I could deal with my own harsh, dry ass reality that I may have missed another recording session. "What you mean? The session isn't until tomorrow night."

"No, Frank, it was last night." Major looked around the messy apartment, spotted a needle and spoon amongst the clutter of sheet music and empty whiskey bottles on the coffee table. He groaned, "What the fuck is goin' on in here? Were you gettin' high all night? I thought we talked about this..."

"Come on, man, don't..." I rubbed the top of my head.

"Is that what you needed the money for? I wouldn't have given it to you if I thought... What the fuck am I saying? Blue, you have a serious problem. I gave you that money to get your horn back from the pawn shop. Where's your damned horn?"

I pointed to my trumpet that was on the floor in the midst of scattered newspapers and records. "I got it from the pawn shop like I said."

He frowned, trying to put the messed up pieces together in his mind. "Then where'd you get the money for this shit then? You went on credit again?"

"Shhhh... Major, you'se fixin' to wake everybody up. They in the room sleeping and you..." I suddenly remembered no one was in the room, so I covered my face to hide my embarrassment.

He looked into the empty bedroom with an even more confused look. "What you talkin' 'bout? Nobody is here but us."

"Never mind…" I shook my head vigorously 'cause my mind quickly reminded me that my family had been gone for a few weeks. *Dammit.* I scratched my arms. My veins craved to feel *more*, but I was out of money… completely broke. I was going to have to either pawn my horn again or get a quick gig. "Look, I'll meet you down for practice. I… I… need to get dressed and things…"

"Are you crazy? You're not gonna practice today. I'm not lettin' you fuck up another note on the same stage as me 'til you let me get you checked into a hospital."

"Come on, man. I don't need to go to a hospital. I'm cool…"

"You're not cool. You need some goddamned help. You're draggin' your words, scratchin', and Frank, you look like shit. You can't be happy with the way things are lookin'? No one will record anything with you like this."

"Plenty of people will record with me," I huffed, feeling offended. "I work my ass off and my passion for my music is still the same."

"Who wants to work with somebody who never shows up and when you do show up, you're hours late? You don't even keep up with the tempo any more. Let me ask you this, if you had to choose between bebop and smack, which would you choose?"

"Aw man, there you go with that bullshit again. I can't have one without the other. You know that, man. I need it to play jazz."

MAJOR JAZZ

"Since when does jazz rely on that shit? Jazz pumps through your veins. Jazz bleeds through your soul, not the drug."

"My soul has been dead for a long time, Major. So long, that it no longer bleeds anything but poison. Just let me do what I do. I don't tell you how to do Major, so you don't tell me how to do Blue!"

With both of his hands in the air, he replied, "You know what? Friends help one another and I'm telling you right now that I'm not going to watch you kill yourself."

"I'm just fine."

"You may be acting all biggity now, but you'll cool down when enough power gets behind you! I'll have you blacklisted from every club in the 'Mo if you don't get your act straight."

"Fuck the 'Mo! I'll take my horn up to... to... to New York."

"And then what? You want to get arrested and spend ten months in jail for narcotics next? Once NYPD gets a hold of you, you'll make the national newspaper. Then when you return to San Francisco, you'll be arrested again, possibly looking at prison time. Does that sound like somethin' you want to do?"

Major was telling the truth. Almost every celebrated jazz musician who was battling drugs had been arrested. With any sign of drug abuse they were getting banned from clubs. Lady Day had got busted at the Mark Twain Hotel downtown San Francisco two years previously, so I knew I had to shape myself up. I was sinking... losing everything I had... and going to jail for awhile wasn't what I wanted next.

"Well, alright now... You made your damned point. I'll get some help."

Niyah Moore

"Good. Now, get some clothes on. I'm taking you right now."

"Right now?" I scowled.

Was he joking? He wanted me to go when I needed one last hit. The thought of the painful process of kicking my habit made me want to die instead. I don't think he understood how sick that was going to make me.

"I'm goin' to New York anyway, with or without you, and I expect you to be clean and sober if you're goin' with me…. Look, I'll quit drinking if you quit."

If he was willing to give up drinking for me, I knew he meant business. It was time to take my music to the next level and get out of San Francisco. I blinked slowly as I tried to think of an alternative way to make him think I was truly clean without actually getting clean, but I knew there was no other way with Major. He only wanted what was best for me. To prove that I could overcome my addiction, I got dressed and checked into the hospital. Once again, my agony flooded in.

I was one tortured soul…

Before then, I was real gone with a woman who was madly in love with me. She was in need of a love that was supreme, an unbinding spell that was tantalizing, forever remarkable, and a classic timeless piece of time that wasn't going to fade easily. Carra Mae Jones *needed* to be loved endlessly, and I wanted to be the man to love her.

The glint of happiness in her eyes when she smiled told me that she adored my syrupy, dark maple-skin that was almost the color of midnight, my pencil-thin mustache, and my bad grade of nappy hair that I laid down with grease and pressed down over night with a stocking cap. It had so many waves you could get seasick. My papa-tree-top six feet height, muscular build, and the way I blew that trumpet from the rotten core of my deep hallowed out soul was what she loved the most.

Yeah, she was digging me.

That was a long time ago. To think, in the beginning, she really didn't want shit to do with me. From the start, she thought I was too cocky, egotistical, and devious, especially when anybody who tried to play their horn while I was in the building ended up at a head-cutting session. I didn't cut anybody slack. I would have them sweating profusely with fast tempo bebop, a real workout, just for the fun of it. For that, she couldn't stand me.

Carra Mae was a girl in the chorus line who waited on tables at the Champagne Supper Club. Out of the five girls, Carra Mae was the darkest in color and shortest in height. The Dancettes were what they were called and the Champagne Supper Club was much like the Hollywood clubs with fancy food, dancing, and floor shows.

They wore uniforms, cute little getups with stockings and heels. The Champagne Supper Club was the place to be if you were among the elite in the 'Mo. While at work, she kept up a professional act. She had no choice really. The owner, Phil, stayed in everyone's business to protect his business, so sneaking around with the Dancettes was supposed to be off limits. Mostly everybody followed the rules or tried to anyway. The rules of the house were made out simple. No play while on the clock.

I was a member of the house band, but I made my own rules, came and went as I pleased, and most certainly dated who I pleased. Rachel, another girl in

Niyah Moore

the Dancettes, was my girlfriend at the time. She had fair skin, long, pretty hair down her back, accompanied by a Colgate white smile that was out of this world. We had a love/hate relationship... broke up every single day like a faucet, off and on.

Rachel barged into my bathroom one morning unannounced. I thought she was gone for the day. "What the fuck is goin' on in here? Blue!"

As much as I wanted to continue to hide my secret from the woman I was involved with, the damned cat was out of the bag.

"Hey baby," I said calmly, taking the needle out of my vein. "What you doin' here? I thought you had rehearsal."

"Phil has been callin' your black ass to get down to the club all mornin'!" Her nostrils flared, tears behind her terrified eyes as she clutched her stomach. "What you in here doin'?"

"It's no big deal, baby. I'll be on my way. Just let me do my thing."

"Fuck you, Blue! I'm done with you! I deal with a lot, but I'm not dealin' with this. I mean to grab the first thing smokin'. You hear me?"

Even after all of the women I cheated on her with and the many fights we had, she never really wanted to leave me. Heroin was her deal breaker. Still, I didn't want her to find out that way. She was gorgeous, but she was also my biggest headache; I couldn't ever get right with her. Like cats and dogs, we fought hard, but we also loved hard. June 11, 1951, she was done with me.

I went down to the club and made up a lie to tell Phil. He didn't care about any excuse I had, just as long as I showed up on time to play. I sat my horn on the bar to get a drink, feeling my high. I felt good.

MAJOR JAZZ

"Lookin' awful pretty there," Tyrone Alley, the drummer, flirted with Carra Mae while he set up on stage.

She had just got done practicing with the Dancettes. She smiled and replied, "Thank you, Tyrone."

After a slight wink from him, she seemed to enjoy his newfound attention toward her as she grinned from ear to ear.

I was drinking and watching Carra Mae from the corner of my eye when Rachel came from the dressing room. She threw her head back as soon as she saw me, rolled her eyes, and walked briskly back in her fancy little getup with an obvious attitude. She was so mad at me for her discovery and I wanted to tell her how sorry I was for making her that way, but my new attraction to Carra Mae wouldn't let me. The insatiable desire to be Carra Mae's lover had me burning like an old furnace.

"What's wrong with Rachel?" Carra Mae asked one of the other girls.

She rubbed her sore legs and tried to whisper, "Her and Frank... they broke up for good this time."

"They're always breaking up. They'll be back together."

I tried to pretend as if I didn't hear them gossiping about me.

"Carra Mae, can I take you out for dinner some time?" That was Tyrone being all flirty.

Tyrone was a clever drummer, part of the talented Alley family. He came from a large family that could play jazz real good. His fraternal twin brother, Tyrell, played the sax. The two of them jigged with anyone who was great.

Niyah Moore

Before she could reply, I interjected, "She doesn't want to go out with you, Sticks."

"Why is that Frank?" Tyrone frowned.

"She's goin' to dinner with me tonight."

Her wide eyes blinked hard as she rebutted, "And what makes you think I want to do somethin' so silly? You got a girl."

"Don't be that way, woman. Frank Blue is no longer taken..." I eyeballed her from head to toe as if I were undressing her.

Rolling her eyes at me, she then turned back to him. "Tyrone, pick me up tonight at eight. You know I stay at my sister's, right?"

A bright smile covered his face as he nodded quickly, "I sure do. I won't be late." His overexcitement made me laugh on the inside... seemed too anxious to me.

"Good." Carra Mae smiled at him before looking me up and down as if I were crazy before going to the dressing room to change.

I could tell by her smirk that she wasn't going to let me get her that easily, but I didn't sweat it. I was going to make her mine in a matter of time. Meanwhile, I had other demons to wrestle.

How did I get into playing the trumpet, you ask? Well, my mama moved to the Western Addition from Georgia to be with her new husband. I was just starting high school. My religious church-going mama was married to a man who worked at the shipyard and they had my little brother, Joe. I didn't know my father. That messed with my head for a long time to see my brother have his daddy. They were this little family and no matter how hard they tried to make me blend, I just wouldn't. I grew to form hate for my step-father, not because he was mean to me, but because he was the kind of man my father wasn't.

I put my focus into music. I played a rented trumpet while in the high school band and was naturally good at it. Learning notes came to me as if I already knew them. Mama thought it would be good to play for the church once I graduated, so I did that until I found other musicians that played in the Fillmo'. I auditioned for my first gig at the Booker T. Washington Center over on Divisadero, nailed it, and joined the Musician's Union like everyone else who played music at that time. She rebuked the devil and threw the Bible in my face every morning, and made me quote scriptures to get me to see that the devil's music was going to send me straight to hell if I didn't repent.

I couldn't get a job on the streetcars because of the color of my damned skin. I was definitely too black to work in the department stores downtown. If you weren't playing an instrument or singing in the 'Mo, you worked at the shipyard or owned your own business. We weren't as fortunate as others, so owning our own business was out of the question. To me, working at the shipyard was like picking cotton. I just wasn't going to do it.

Music made me feel too alive to just give it up for religious reasons. Behind her back, I played all over the city with different people, worked seven days a week for eight dollars a night and ended up at the Champagne Supper Club. I made sure I went to church every Sunday to please her, but once I got my own place on McAllister, I stopped going all together 'cause it conflicted with my nights at the Champagne Supper Club. Fillmo' was the only place where people made me feel like a superstar, especially after I started touring in New York. Music paid very well and people recognized me.

My range of trumpet techniques was more than just extended. I rolled the tip of my tongue to produce growling-like tones as if I were rolling an *R* sound, and simultaneously hummed while playing a note that created two sets of vibrations that interfered with one another. Many jazz players used that technique, but with my flutter-tonguing, I modified the sound.

Ta-ka ta-ka ta-ka... I articulated using those syllables.

Ta-ta-ka ta-ta-ka ta-ta-ka... I triple tongued those syllables.

When I doodle-tongued my notes while improvising, as if saying the word doodle, the temperature in the atmosphere always changed. Women fanned themselves and the house was on their feet. I slid between notes, depressed each valve halfway, and changed my lip tension from fast, slow, or no vibrato to actual rhythmic patterns with vibrato. By hissing, clicking, or simply breathing, my trumpet was made to resonate in ways that didn't sound like a trumpet at all, much like a woman having a frantic fit during an orgasm.

Jazz and my lady should've been the only two things that consumed me, but I was introduced to the one thing that became my poison when I was young. When I was playing a few shows in New York City, at eighteen, I saw what heroin did to some cats out there. It was sad the way they were strung out, selling everything they owned worth value. I thought, *Nah that would never happen to me.*

Leo, a bass player from Brooklyn, had the smack and had a crafty way with peer pressure. "You want to sound like Bird, don't you?"

MAJOR JAZZ

"Man, I sound better than Charlie Parker. Plus, he ain't doin' junk."

"Trust me… Bird's doin' it. You have to have some junk so you can sound like Bird."

Charlie Parker, Bird, was the man. Everyone knew he was an addict. He was playing illegally 'cause he got busted for narcotics. I didn't want to do it to sound like him and I definitely didn't want anyone to think I was a junkie.

"A lot of jazz musicians are doing it. It will enhance your talent and make you feel *good* with just a little bit," he pressed.

Hell, I had been feeling real down and depressed because something was missing in my life. My father's absence played a big role in my depression. That downright miserable feeling was something I couldn't shake. My faith in God only comforted me to a degree.

"Will it make me take my mind off my troubles?"

"Just like that." He snapped his finger.

"Give me just a little then. I don't want to look like nobodies junkie. You hear me?"

"Yeah man, I hear you. I'm your friend. I wouldn't steer you wrong," Leo said.

I watched him get the needle ready. I hated needles. Squirming in my skin, I scowled, "Man, is this the only way?"

"This is the only way to hit you in a hurry. I know some that put it up their noses…"

I didn't want to shove anything up my nose. I closed my eyes so I wouldn't have to see the needle pierce my skin and sat at the table while he fixed me up. The first time I felt heroin shoot up my veins it made my skin crawl, burned a little, but it relaxed me

Niyah Moore

instantly just like he said. It took my mind off any and everything. Heroin became Jazz and Jazz became heroin. They became one in the same, replacing my insecurities with confidence.

Once back in San Francisco, the anticipation of that good feeling had me on a hunt. It wasn't too hard to find. My friend Johnnie had it. Once I got it, I became that motherfucker they called Blue.

Carra Mae was perfect, but if I didn't hear Sticks asking her out that day, I wouldn't have felt challenged to try to get to her before he could. Carra Mae wasn't movie star beautiful like Rachel. Carra Mae was the shy girl next door kind of beautiful and there was something about her naïve innocence that intrigued me most. I thought it would be an easy battle to get Carra Mae to fall in love with me, but boy was I wrong.

Though she shot me down like a military plane gunned down by the enemy, I managed to avoid the blazing crash by using my emergency parachute-- my charm. If she thought I was going to let Sticks beat me to taking her out, she had another thing coming.

I showed up at her sister's place to take her out for dinner, dressed in my finest suit and long coat with a box of See's chocolates and roses. After she opened the door, she stared at me through narrowed eyes as if I were an alien on her porch. She folded her arms across her chest and looked at me like she truly wanted to slap me. "Where the hell is Tyrone?"

"He got sick and didn't want to disappoint you, so he sent me over to cover for him."

With her eyes turning into small slits, she nearly yelled, "You're a horrible liar, Frank Blue, and I'm not goin' anywhere with you!"

I smiled at her cute sass to play off the shunned feeling. "Say, little lady, why don't you get your fine self in my automobile so I can take you some place nice?"

"Why don't you get off my porch and call your girlfriend Rachel?"

"Rachel isn't my lady."

Carra Mae kept her arms folded across her chest. "How can I be so sure 'bout that?"

"I'm a one woman kind of man, sweetheart."

She looked at me up and down, silently arguing with her own stubborn mind, real hesitant, knowing my truth. I didn't know the meaning of true commitment, but no woman wants to hear the absolute truth no matter what they say. She was no exception to the rule. She looked down the street as if Tyrone was going to magically appear any minute.

"He's not coming, baby doll."

"What you do to him?"

I chuckled. "Sticks is just fine. I can assure you that he sent me."

I tried to hand her the gift wrapped box of chocolates and roses, but she stared at them with uncertainty as she shifted all of her weight to her left leg. "Good night, Frank." Without another word, she closed the door on me.

I walked down the steps of the porch, looked at the front door, calmly put my left hand in my slack's pocket, and leaned up against my car. I wasn't going to leave just because she wanted me to and I was going to prove how serious I was about taking her out.

After a minute or two, she poked her head out. "What you still doing here?"

"I'm not goin' anywhere 'til you go out with me."

Her lips parted as if she was going to say something rude, but she blew out a little air instead, shaking her head at me. "I'm not going with you."

Niyah Moore

"I'll wait all night 'til the sun comes up if I have to."

"Why would you do somethin' so stupid?"

When I winked at her, she slammed the door that time.

I watched every light inside of her sister's place turn off. I frowned a little because I wasn't used to women giving me the cold shoulder. *Was I attractive enough? Did she care that much about Rachel's feelings?* She had truly stumped me. I rested the gifts on the hood of the car and lit a Camel cigarette. By the time I finished smoking, she still hadn't come outside. Damn, I was going to have to try my luck one more time another time. Just when I was about to get into my car and leave, she came out with her coat on. While she locked up, I opened the passenger door for her with a slight smile.

"You might as well wipe that silly grin off your face. This is one date, Frank, and one date only."

She took the box of chocolates and roses as soon as she was inside of the car.

I walked to the driver's side and got in knowing that this wouldn't be our last date. As I pulled away from the curb, she asked, "Where are we going for dinner?"

"I have this little restaurant in mind. I'm in the mood for some seafood. Do you like crab?"

"I like crab... How come you and Rachel ain't goin' to dinner tonight?"

I don't know why that woman was wondering about another woman. Instead of enjoying the moment for what it was, she wanted to figure out my relationship with Rachel. Typical woman shit.

"You don't have to worry 'bout her."

"Why'd you sit outside for almost half an hour?"

"I think you're pretty. I like the way your face lights up when you smile."

She tried to hold her smile back as she bit on her lower lip, but it wasn't working. "Thank you."

I gave her the royal treatment and spent a good deal of money that night. After eating crab, drinking champagne, and laughing for a few hours, I took her home. I ended the evening with a kiss on her hand and made sure she got into her house safe.

Tyrone Alley was a little bit of a sore loser. He bet five dollars that I couldn't pull off a good date and was mad for losing out on a good woman, but after awhile he got used to seeing us together. Rachel quit the Dancettes as soon as she found out about us and moved to Alabama with family. Phil replaced Rachel with another girl. It seemed like as soon as one quit or was fired, he had another girl lined up the very same day.

It wasn't long before Carra Mae started spending a few nights with me out of the week. After late night shows, we would make love and stay up for hours talking until we both fell asleep. After a few short weeks, I asked her to move in. Being with her felt like breathing fresh, crisp air. With her around, I didn't have the urge to get high but every once in a while to get a little taste. She didn't argue or nag me about jam sessions running over into the wee hours of the morning and she knew how to cook everything I liked. I didn't know a city-bred woman could cook like she was from the Bam. She knew how to thicken a lean brother up.

"Baby, you want some more collard greens?"

"I'm so full. I can't take another bite," I replied, pushing the plate away.

Niyah Moore

A few band members came over for dinner whenever she cooked. Major was in our company that night along with them damned Alley Cats. We were drinking hooch and reminiscing on the first time we met at Bop City when we were teenagers.

"Do you 'member how I pissed Jim off when he found out how old I was?" Major asked before producing a hearty laugh from his gut.

We all laughed. Shit, the teen years seemed so long ago, but we were barely hitting our mid-twenties.

"None of us had any business being up in there," I said.

Major gulped his drink. He was an alcoholic, though he wouldn't admit it. I don't think I ever really saw him sober around that time.

"Would anyone else like some more of anything?" Carra Mae asked.

"I'll have some more cornbread," Tyrell said.

"Me too," Tyrone added, "and another short rib, if there's any left."

"I'll take a little more greens," Major replied. "You sure are lucky, Blue. She really can cook."

I pat my stomach. "You see I'm gettin' fat around here. She's a kitchen mechanic, too... Hey Major, how are things comin' with that new singer?"

"Candy Cane Taylor is comin' along."

"How she sound?"

"She sounds like pure sugar so sweet. You should come perform on her first night at the Primalon Ballroom tomorrow night."

"You got it." I lifted my glass to his.

Our glasses clinked before we drank some more.

"I saw Ginger down at Club Alabam last night," Tyrone said to Major. "Are you still layin' it to her?"

MAJOR JAZZ

Major took a mouthful of greens, chewed, and swallowed before he replied, "Ginger is down with me."

"So is Sallie Aquino," Tyrell pointed out. "Boy, I tell you, you must be tired from all those miles. How do you bounce between two women like that?"

"You must be sugar curin' the ladies' feelings."

Those damned Alley Cats were always trying to figure out the game of women. They never experienced the swarm like we did. Women threw themselves at our feet like we were gods. It was crazy sometimes.

"Watch carefully and you might learn somethin'." Major winked.

"I'm crackin', but I'm fackin'," Tyrell added.

He was wise-cracking, but telling the truth. We all laughed with him.

"I'm sure Major can never get tired of entertaining the ladies. He's so natural at it," Carra Mae said, putting in her two cents.

Major chuckled. "That's a hell of an observation lil' lady, but don't believe everything your eyes tell you."

"You can't help that you're a heartbreaker."

"I don't think I'm a heartbreaker. Well, at least, I haven't heard that. Sallie and Ginger know that I can never love them the way they want me to and I don't pretend as if I do when I don't. They fool with me at their own risk. Music rules this heart and as long as it does, a woman will never be able to win."

Carra Mae hummed while she cleared the plates from the table that were no longer in use. As soon as she left out of the dining room I whispered to Major, "You can't be talkin' like that in front of her."

Major laughed. "Why not? You think she actually believes that you're not a dog anymore?"

"I'm not dogging her."

Niyah Moore

"Not yet anyway," Tyrone said.

I laughed at Tyrone. "You still sore over losing her, Sticks?"

"I have a woman," he replied quickly.

"Then why you over there beatin' up your gums?"

We all laughed.

"You won that bet fair and square. I have to give it to you," Tyrone declared.

Silence fell on the room because Carra Mae was back to clear more dishes.

"What bet you win fair and square?" Carra Mae stood over me.

I wrapped my arm around her waist. "Man stuff, baby. A small card game is all."

She pushed me away gently. "Mmmmm... Y'all finish on up so I can clean this mess up. I'm 'bout ready to go to bed."

"Are you gonna play for me tomorrow night? Candy Cane Taylor's first show and I want you to guest spot," Major said again as if he didn't ask already. Whenever he got drunk, he tended to ask the same question a few times.

"I told you yes already. I'll be there."

"Good. Be there on time."

I helped Carra Mae tidy the table to clear up the smoke just in case she heard what the bet had been about. If she heard, she didn't let on that she knew anything about it. The fellas stumbled out the door, all too inebriated, making instrument sounds with their mouths in perfect harmony as they walked down the street.

"Baby, you ready for bed?" she asked, turning off the kitchen light.

My mind was too heavy for sleep. I wanted to play a little bit before I closed my eyes anyway. I picked up my trumpet and pressed the valves. "Not right now. Will my blowing keep you up?"

"No. Sounds like my lullaby. What you gonna play?"

"You have any requests?"

"Anything you choose is fine with me, baby."

I smiled at her. "I think I'll play somethin' new I'm writing."

"What's it called?"

"Something Kind of Blue. I just came up with it the other day."

She frowned, scrunching up her nose. "That sounds sad."

"It's the blues, baby. It's supposed to sound a little sad."

"Alright." With a sweet kiss, she left me alone to my thoughts and my horn.

My mother had just been diagnosed with Cancer and with the sickness spreading and eating up her body, I felt helpless. I wanted to save her, but if the medicine the doctors had given her wasn't going to cure her terminal illness, I wasn't sure how I would be able to handle it. I put the trumpet to my lips and played the first note of the scale, Middle C, by holding no valves down and blowing into the mouthpiece. With my eyes closed, I played what I felt in my soul. The emptiness never seemed to go away and though it came out into the song I wrote, it remained. I wanted to know who my father was, as grown as I was. I had too many unanswered questions. *Did my mother know who he was? She was fifteen when she had me... did he rape her? Did he ever come looking for me? Was he dead or alive?* I had asked my mother over a million times and her answer was always the same.

"I'm your mother *and* father, boy. What you want with him?"

Once I played myself tired, I curled up in bed with my woman. I never let her see how much my eyes spilled tears before getting into bed or how much pain my heart had been in, but she could feel it in the way I played that horn with enough pain to permeate the deepest sea.

"You feel better now, baby?"

I squeezed her tighter, without words. She felt my emptiness. She felt my pain. She knew I needed her. Without her I would drown in my own sorrow.

Frank

"Major! Where are you, you crazy ass nigger?" That was Ginger, barging in on our dress rehearsal as if she had been invited.

Major, immediately, stopped playing the piano, hopped down from the stage to stop her from causing a scene, and grabbed her arm so roughly that they began to tussle a bit.

"Take your hands off me! You lied to me, you cheating ass bastard! You lied to me!" She hollered and cried like a crazy mad woman, swinging at him all the while.

Pulling her outside, he left me alone with them damned Alley Cats.

"Y'all sure this show is goin' on tonight? Seems like Miss Ginger is pissed off," I said, cradling my horn.

Tyrone shook his head. "Major done got his ass in hot water now. Ginger doesn't like the idea of Miss Sallie dressing Candy Cane and all. I told him he should've just told her the word from the bird."

Tyrell added, "That's why I don't cross two women. No sir, I married Mary out of high school and that's where I'm staying."

"Marriage is some heavy business, so you better stay your ass right there," I chuckled.

"You plan on marrying Carra Mae?" Tyrone asked.

He was always so worried about Carra Mae. I believe if I would've turned my back and messed up in any sort of way, he would've been right there to pick up the pieces. I believed he liked her too much, but he wouldn't admit it.

"If she'll have me, then yes, I'll make an honest woman out of her," I answered.

"Of course, she'll have you. What are you saying? Do you want to marry her?"

He was insistent on pulling that information out of me. I didn't want to bite off something I couldn't chew. As if with perfect timing, my friend Johnnie came in through the front door, so I excused myself from the stage to meet him backstage. The twins stared at one another as if they were talking in some sort of secret silent twin language they had. I didn't worry about them.

Johnnie was the only dealer that I could rely on and though he was married to Sallie Aquino's sister, Lucille, I had to make sure he got there before Sallie did. I paid him and he hooked me up with a keen enough dose to get me through the rest of the day.

By the time I got back on stage, Major was back at the piano, Ginger was sitting in the front row, and Sallie was coming through the front door with a look of unease on her face and I knew what that meant. She had seen Johnnie leaving, but she seemed to be more worried about Ginger sitting in the front row. Sallie went backstage and carried on without saying a word.

"One, two, one, two, three, four!" Major shouted to get us back to practicing.

***

We had a great show that night at the Primalon Ballroom. Candy Cane Taylor was the neighborhood's newest star due to her powerful first performance. Major threw one of his infamous after-show house parties. Plus, Candy had been offered to record a single

in Los Angeles. That meant a big deal to Major, so a celebration was only appropriate.

Major found me in a corner with Carra Mae. I wore sunglasses, so others wouldn't see just how loaded I truly was. "Excuse me, Mae. Can I please have a word with Frank?"

"Sure..."

"Come with me while I smoke a Camel," Major said.

I followed him on outside. "What's on your mind, Daddy-O?"

He lit a cigarette. "Sallie mentioned somethin' 'bout seeing her brother-in-law, Johnnie, leavin' the Ballroom this mornin'. We all know Johnnie is one of the neighborhood's dealers. You want to tell me what that was about?"

"Johnnie owed me some money," I replied. I already had my lie together.

Major lowered his voice in case someone would unexpectedly walk up. "Look, I know you were backstage with Johnnie and I don't think it was about money. I know Sallie's assumptions about the situation could be off, but it just seems kinda like... "

"So, are you askin' me or tellin' me what you think you know?"

"There's a difference in your playin'... Your tempo has changed, not in a bad way... different. I've played with you long enough to know your sound and you look like you're blitzed right now if you ask me."

"Johnnie is one of my good friends. I got into a lil' gamblin' bet with him and he came to pay me for his loss."

Major narrowed his eyes and studied the way I kept those sunglasses on in the night time. He could tell I was loaded and right when he was about to give it to me straight, Carra Mae came outside.

"I'm tired, Frank. You ready to go home?"

"I'm ready if you are, baby doll," I answered.

"I'm ready now," she whined. Liquor made her whiney at times, especially when she was getting sleepy.

"Well, alright now, Major. Be easy. I'll talk to you later."

I slid him some skin.

***

"Baby, you feelin' alright?" she asked as I drove on the white line in the middle of the street. When I didn't respond, she questioned, "You need me to drive?"

"Yeah, I need you to drive. I'm not feeling too well."

"What's the matter? Are you drunk?"

"Just drive for me." I pulled over to the curb and got out slowly, careful not to loose my balance.

We switched places and she drove us home. I could feel my high coming down and I wasn't ready to come down. I wanted to keep the good feeling going. My mind was thinking about calling Johnnie for some more, but then I remembered I had some stashed away in the medicine cabinet. Once home, I immediately went into the bathroom. A sweet sensation occurred after I depressed the heroin off into my vein to cross my blood-brain barrier and it flooded me with warmth, relief, and a pleasurable rush.

Carra Mae was on her way to take a bath because she never got into the bed dirty. On her way, she took notice of me nodding while standing up against the wall. "Babe…" She put her arms around my waist and tried to look into my eyes, only they were closed. "What's goin' on with you?" She searched my

arms for a sign of her suspicion. She found the track marks. I had done it enough times for scarring and toxin buildup to produce tracks along the length of my veins.

"Let's get you into bed."

I groaned and moaned as she guided me to the bedroom where I collapsed on the bed and slept in my clothes.

When I woke up, it was in the middle of the day, and Carra Mae was staring down at me with worry nestled underneath her teary eyes. "How long, Frank?"

"How long, Frank, what?"

"How long have you been shootin' up?"

"I ain't been shootin' up. Don't be silly."

"I had a feelin'... I talked to Major a few minutes ago... He wants me to keep an eye on you 'cause he thinks you're using... I didn't know your friend Johnnie was bad news."

"He ain't bad news."

"Is he a drug dealer, Frank?"

"Johnnie ain't bad news. He's one of my good friends. Major is worried about nothin'."

"Is he a drug dealer, Frank?" she repeated.

I shrugged. "Shit, he might be..." Chills suddenly covered my body as if the window was wide open and the bay's air invaded me. I sat on the edge of the bed and my legs started shaking up and down, like a surge of nervous energy. I closed my eyes and tried to relax, holding my breath. I scratched my arms and that brought on a wave of slight euphoria and a recharge. When I opened my eyes, Carra Mae was still staring at me.

"Baby, if you think I don't know what a junkie looks like, then you must think I'm truly dumb as a doorknob... You, baby, are startin' to look like a junkie."

MAJOR JAZZ

"Where's my horn?" I jumped up, ignoring her, and went into the living room, feeling the urge to play.

She followed me with her soft words trailing me, "I love you, Frank. You know you don't have to get doped up. All you have to do is lay it on me, baby. Tell me what's goin' on with you…"

I stared at how sincere she was being. "Will you leave me if I don't stop?"

Tears streaked her face because my confession pained her. "As long as you keep puttin' that poison in your system, you'll lose me. I can't sit around and watch you do this to yourself. Yes, I'll pack my bags and go. I mean that."

I believed her. The thought of her leaving scared me. Nothing was worth her leaving me.

"Baby, baby, baby," I pleaded, falling to my knees. "Please, don't leave me. I'll give it up for you."

"Not just for me, Frank, but for the both of us…"

That was the first time I decided to get clean. I didn't go to a rehab center. I figured I could kick the habit at home. Those were the worst nights of my life. What helped was that she didn't leave my side.

My stomach cramped in this unbearable pain, constipation had it in knots. I couldn't stop sweating profusely and soaked the bed while I tossed and turned. Sleep escaped me. I threw up so much my stomach pains worsened. Every bone in my body felt achy, my skin felt clammy, and I couldn't stop myself from kicking and punching the air because my nerves were doing something insanely crazy. Nobody said "kicking" the habit would be easy and it took Carra Mae to help me not to relapse just to get over being so sick.

I felt like I was dying...

I prayed to God. *Lord, if you help me through this, I'll never get high again.*

Niyah Moore

***

I had been clean for a good six months when Carra Mae was expecting our first child. She took some time off from work at the Champagne Supper Club. She kept our ship sailing smooth while taking care of our home. My gigs were constant and it seemed as if everyone I ran into congratulated me on kicking my bad habit. It was strange how no one acted like they noticed my habit before I got clean. Smiling at them, I was truly feeling in a better place.

Major was especially happy that I was drug free and asked me, "Say Blue, why don't you join me for a few nights in Harlem? I got a nice gig lined up."

I didn't hesitate because I had a baby on the way and money was tight, I needed more money to take care of my family. "Let's go."

Every time I went to New York it was sweet and the pay was more than grand. It was our first time in New York together. We drank hard, partied hard, and jammed harder from club to club. Beautiful women swarmed all over the place in their fancy dresses, fur coats, and jewels. Major and I could barely go anywhere without a few women begging to get into the bed with us. Our hotel suites had become something like Pussy Palace, so we took full advantage of what was given to us freely.

Life was sweet. Things didn't come unraveled for me until I ran into Leo at the Waffle House, the man who introduced me to heroin years before.

Major was on his way out of the door to go lay up with a lady. "See you in the morning, Blue."

"Lata Alligata," I called to him while I stared my demon in the face. Leo looked like a million bucks with his gold rings shining and tailored made expensive looking suit. He traded his bass in for another life. The drug business had treated him like a King Pin.

"Hey Blue, it's good to see you in town. I heard you had a good show tonight."

I brushed him off casually, tipping my hat towards him without speaking. That didn't stop Leo from sitting at my table as if he had been invited. A few ladies were in my company along with a few of the band members, so I tried not to look uneasy as I chewed on a toothpick.

"So, what's new?" he asked with a sly grin crossing his face.

"Music. That's always new. I'm getting on some stiff time."

"I dig that. My bass playin' days are over. Say, come outside and smoke with me."

I paid the dinner bill and got up to leave. "No can do, Leo. I have a flight in the morning. You have a good night, you hear?"

"Here, take my number if you need *anything* before you leave." Leo left his card on the table.

My heart was racing and my heart sped up, pushing all the blood to rush through me so fast. The temptation was right there. I was strong enough to watch him walk away without thinking much about anything other than going about my own business. The thought was to rip up the card and toss it, but for some reason I didn't. I put it in my jacket's pocket, just in case, and walked out of the Waffle House.

Back in my hotel room, I packed my clothes in my suitcase and then called Major to confirm the time of the flight. I took a shower with a lady I met that night, sexed her, sent her on her way, and tried to go to sleep. The middle of the night hadn't been kind to me because my mind was on calling Leo. It betrayed me while I tossed and turned. I had a full on conversation with my thoughts. *You don't need it, man... Yes, you do... Life is fine without it... All you need is just a little taste... No, you don't... Oh, but how good it feels. Yes, how good it feels... Don't you miss it?*

I yearned to feel the drug that released my pain or just to get a little taste. That's all I really needed, just a little taste. It was like craving to have your favorite dessert in the middle of the night while trying to be on a diet. If I wouldn't have seen Leo, I probably wouldn't have had that thought in my head. I crept to the edge of the bed slowly, sat up, rubbed my face, and took in a deep breath. Getting up to go to the bathroom, I exhaled and argued with myself some more. *Come on, Blue. Man, you don't need it. Yes, you do...*

Splashing cold water on my face, I thought that would do the trick to stop me from wanting to get high. With nervous hands and heart pounding, I lost the battle with my mind. I went ahead and called him.

I spent all night, nodding, but everything fled my mind. When it came time to get back on the plane to go home, I wished I would've gotten on a later flight. Self-reproach set in.

Major took one look at me and knew it. "Aw, damn, Frank," he said as we filed through the airport terminal.

"Major... I... I fucked up." I didn't blame it on anyone. My relapse was completely my fault.

He shook his head at me. "I shouldn't have left you alone last night. Somethin' told me not to... Man, you can't go home to Carra Mae like this. She's gonna know for sure you fucked up. You have to stay at my place a few days under my close supervision."

"Okay, man... Thanks..."

MAJOR JAZZ

For two days, I slept at Major's.

Once I was done beating myself up about it, I went home. I closed the front door behind me, leaving my suitcases by the door. "Baby, your man is home." I took off my coat and hung it up on the coat rack. The nervousness in my stomach hoped she wouldn't be able to detect my secret.

She met me in the hallway and we embraced. I kissed her instantly because I missed her so much. Readily accepting my greeting, she said, "I made you a pie, baby. You want some?"

"What kind of pie you make for me?"

"I made your favorite, sweet potato."

I bit on my lower lip and kissed her again. That was indeed my favorite pie. Pie always made me feel somewhat better. I flashed my smile before replying, "I'm gonna get washed up first."

"Okay, I want to hear all about the excitement in New York." She giggled and went to the kitchen.

I walked down the narrow hallway to the bathroom, splashed cool water on my face to rid me of more guilt, and then relieved my bladder. She hadn't suspected a thing at first glance and that was good. When I returned to her presence, a nice slice of pie was waiting for me with a cold glass of milk. That woman knew just what I liked. She paid attention to the smallest details, and for that I loved her even more. I sat at the head of the table and picked up the fork to dig in.

"How was the Big Apple?" Her eyes lit up with fascination from across the table with her own slice.

"Baby, the New York jazz scene is happenin'. We played at The Five Spot near Astor Place and bebop is expanding there. It was amazin'. Miles Davis and Charles Mingus stopped through there. Talk about jammin' and the house was packed." I whistled before taking a bite of the pie. It melted the way sweet potato pie was supposed to as soon as it touched my tongue. Oh, I could taste the vanilla and cinnamon. That pie was made with love and it showed. "This is some damned good pie, baby."

"I'm glad you like it. What else y'all do while there?"

"We went over to Birdland to check out Charlie Parker and his band. The place was crowded... seats five hundred with a long bar, tables, booths, and a spot for an orchestra. It's outta sight. Have you ever been there?"

"No, I've never left San Francisco."

"One day, I'm gonna take you there. You'll love it."

That heavenly slice of pie was finished in no time. As she came to take my plate, I pulled her down to sit on my lap. We indulged in some heavy kissing. The way her lips felt on mine made me wish I never went to New York.

"You kiss me like you missed me," she giggled, kissing me repeatedly.

"Let me show you just how much." I held her tight before lifting her up and carrying her to the bedroom.

Carra Mae may have been a timid woman, but when it came down to getting the job done in the bedroom, she was far from timid. She was at ease with having sex and the kind of sex I liked to have -- passionate and rough. When it came to providing that long felt need, she was in a class by herself. No one could lay it to me like she could.

Her hands roamed my body freely while I undressed. As she made her way up and down my arms, she stopped when she felt the line of bruised needle holes in my left arm. It usually took a week for them to go away if not replenished by fresh injections, so the ones in my good vein had yet to heal.

What I had done in New York had come out of the shadows and stepped into the light. I tried to kiss her before she could start asking questions, but she backed away slightly.

"Frank Blue... you want to tell me what else you were up to while in New York?"

"What you talkin' about woman?" I removed my eyes from her.

"Look at me, Frank." She turned my face to hers.

There were visible welling tears in my eyes when I finally looked at her. My sadness made her anger dissipate. My struggle was one she didn't understand, but she was trying. Instead of scolding me, she held me, kissed me, and cried with me. My pain was like the roots of a dead tree. She wasn't sure just how deep my stems were, but she wanted to do her best to help dig them up -- a laborious task. I was afraid I would slowly break apart, decompose, and become part of the soil, but she wasn't going to go for that. She was determined to leave bare workable ground.

***

Our son, Frank Jr. was born and life seemed to be headed in the right direction. I was heroin free, but I started drinking more to replace it. I was elated to be a father. I had to be in my son's life because my father wasn't around. His life seemed to be enough to make me appreciate my own and to stay clean. My mother was also excited about being a grandmother.

Gig after gig, I heated up stages night after night in the 'Mo. I never had to wait for a table or pay for much. I was treated like royalty. Everybody who was anybody knew me.

At home, Carra Mae juggled taking care of the baby, cooked meals, cleaned the house, and gave great sex. I really didn't have anything to complain about. Our son was growing healthy and strong. What more could a man ask for?

I wanted to show her my appreciation. "Tonight, I want you to relax, Carra Mae. I'll clean up the dishes all by myself. I want you to kick your feet up on the couch and just relax."

"I don't believe you."

I smiled at her. "Sit down and take a load off."

"You do somethin' you feel guilty about?"

I chuckled at her. "No. I just want to show my appreciation. Is that alright with you?"

She untied her apron, hung it up behind the kitchen door, and flopped down on the couch. "That is more than fine with me. The baby is asleep and I can have some quiet time." The grin on her face said a million thank yous.

After I had the kitchen sparkling, I joined her on the couch. With my head resting on her full breasts, she caressed the top of my head and said, "Frank…"

With my eyes closed I answered, "Hmmm?"

"I think I'm pregnant again."

I looked up into her eyes. Frank, Jr. was all but ten months old or something. "What?"

"I found out this morning… You're goin' to be a daddy again."

Two babies?

I smiled at her, even though worry filled me. I was just getting used to the idea of just the three of us, and now Carra Mae was pregnant again. Sudden changes never did sit well with me.

Frank

B lue baby, it's so good to see you." That was the owner of the Blue Mirror, Miss Leola, welcoming me into her nightclub that was decorated with molded Greek figurines on the walls, a circular bar, and blue velvet garlands surrounding the place.

Playing at the Blue Mirror was like playing in a thug's paradise. Gambling, drinking, reefer, winos, prostitutes, and anything else illegal you wanted to find was up in that spot. Miss Leola only rolled with the high rollers and most of her friends were hustlers, street peddlers, and pimps in sharkskin suits, alligator shoes, and diamond watches. Drug dealers and hoodlums saturated the Blue Mirror every night of the week.

Whenever Miss Leola wasn't running her nightclub, she was seen cruisin' down Fillmore Street in a Cadillac with her husband who was known for working closely with the mob. Leola's vivacious personality spoke for itself and everyone was drawn to her. One thing was for sure, she had the loudest mouth I had ever heard on a woman. "Get up here, Blue! Play somethin' for us, baby!"

"Not tonight…"

"Oh, come on. John Coltrane is in here. Maybe you can duet."

Ah, John Coltrane. That was before he became the Trane. He was fresh on the Fillmo' scene and his popularity was growing more rampant the more he played around town. He had already made a name for himself in New York. Though that duet would've played out nice, I had other things on my mind.

I wasn't there to play my horn... I was looking to score. Johnnie was in jail again, so I couldn't call him. With Carra Mae's news of being pregnant again, she had a Negro stressed out to the max. Getting high was the only thing I wanted to do to help appease me. Liquor alone couldn't quiet my troubled mind the way I wanted it to. T-Bone Walker was on stage with his band, the Rhythm Rockers, and the place was truly rockin'.

I was still scanning the room for a familiar face when this young woman kept coming in and out of the club as if she were looking for somebody in particular. She was quite distracting, built like a double order of pancakes, sweet and stacked, with her incandescent platinum hair curled on top of her head elegantly. Her skin was the color of a honey coated graham cracker. I had seen her a few times, but only at the Blue Mirror. The way her red dress clung to her body had my full attention. My eyes went to her legs next because they were long and so soft looking as she sauntered in those heels.

She walked straight over to me, as if I was the man she had been looking for all along, brushed her plump breasts against my chest, and handed me a thick roll of money. "Here, take this."

I unrolled the wad and hundreds unfolded. "How'd you get all this bread lil' lady?"

She told me to come closer with her index finger. I bent down to hear her as she whispered in my ear, "I'm a hooker, sweetie. You know what that is?"

I nodded. She was too beautiful to be a hooker, but that was her way of making her ends meet and she was sexy enough to get away with it. As badly as I wanted to take her money, I knew that would make me her pimp and I wasn't into that. I handed it back to her just

Niyah Moore

as smoothly as she had handed it to me. "You've got the wrong man, baby doll."

"I like you." She licked her lips, placed the roll into her bra, and winked at me before sauntering over to the other side of the room.

I moved my eyes around to see if I could ask someone where I could find some junk. I didn't see anyone I knew that well and wasn't going to just ask around. Asking the wrong person would lead to someone possibly calling the wagon. Getting kicked out of the Musician's Union was the last thing I needed.

"Let me get some whiskey," I ordered and sat at the bar for a little while. My next plan was to just go home if I couldn't score.

When I was almost finished with my drink, the same sexy young woman with the platinum hair was making her way back to me. She questioned, "You find what you're lookin' for?"

I took hold of her arm gently. "Say, baby, you know where I can score?"

A sly smile graced her face as she licked her teeth. "Follow me."

My first mind was on not following her, in case someone would think I was trying to pay her for her sex, but then my second mind didn't give a fuck. If she had the goods, then I wanted what she had.

She linked arms with me and we hopped in a taxi cab on over to the Ellis Hotel. She took me to a room she had already checked into. That was her place of residence for a few nights.

"Sit," she ordered.

Reluctantly, I sat on the bed. I wasn't sure if she remembered why I was there. She removed her dress, walked around the room in just her bra and panty, and confusion really set in. Did she think I was asking to have jelly? If so, she had the wrong idea.

"Hey…"

She cut me off. "Trust me, baby. You're lookin' to get high, right?" She reached under the bed and pulled out a suitcase full of her clothing before producing what I was looking for.

I relaxed, but just a little bit. Why did she have to get undressed to get high? And why did she have so much of it?

"Are you a dealer, too?"

"No… This is mine." Judging by the amount she had, I knew there was no doubt in my mind that one of her best customers was a dealer and had fixed her up with enough to have a grand party. I watched her break some down and snort it up her nose from the back of her hand. "Here, take a hit."

"Oh no, I don't do it that way."

"So, you're a pin cushion? You're too cute to be a pin cushion, baby. Why don't you try it this way? I don't have any needles and melting it down takes too long." She rolled up a dollar bill and made a few lines. She demonstrated how to do it.

Handing me the rolled up dollar, she said, "Your turn."

I did it the way she showed me, inhaling the first line.

"Now, do these two," she suggested. "You're a heavy hitter."

At first, I didn't feel anything until it drained down the back of my throat. Though, I didn't like the taste of it, I could feel the drug entering my system very slowly, too slowly. When shooting up, I usually felt the rush immediately. I had to do more. I lay back on the bed and closed my eyes to try to enjoy the slow creep.

Niyah Moore

The young woman stared at me seductively through lowered eyes before she straddled me. She truly looked foxy.

I didn't protest, but I said, "I'm not paying you for jelly."

"You don't have to pay me. This isn't business, baby. This is my pleasure. Like I said earlier, I like you."

"Dig that..."

She kissed me sensually. My hands caressed her body and she moaned. It wasn't long before we were both naked and our shared high intensified the moment I entered into her wet center. Her core was just as rotten as mine, I could feel it. She sold her body for sex to cover up her insecurities and she really just wanted somebody to love her. She chose me to be the man to love her.

After we were done, I asked, "What's your name, beauty?"

"Liz." Her smile was warm and she seemed like a normal girl, unlike the sex-driven goddess I had encountered earlier in the evening.

"My name is-"

"I know who you are," she cut me off. "Blue. Let's just say, I've had my eye on you for a while. Hopefully, I'll see you again."

She had the smack, sex, and plenty of bread. I was ready to ride her ride whenever she wanted me to. "You'll see me again."

"You got a chick at home?"

I nodded. "Yes."

"Kids?"

"I have a son and another one on the way."

"Lucky lady."

MAJOR JAZZ

"I wouldn't call her lucky. I mean, look at where I am right now. She's at home taking care of the baby, thinking I'm playing a gig..."

She left my side and went over to her purse to take out some money. "Take this to her. That way, she'll believe your story."

I was too high to deny her. Everything about that night felt good. She felt good. The bread was good. So, I went ahead and took it from her.

That was how Liz and I began.

***

For months, hanging out at the Blue Mirror had become a part of my bad habit between gigs and home life. Our son turned one and Carra Mae was getting further along in the pregnancy. I took one last look at myself in the mirror, sprayed on some smell goods, and put on my hat and coat.

Carra Mae eyeballed my attire, which wasn't anything fancier than the way I usually dressed when going to a gig, but she decided to pick a fight with me. "You gonna fool 'round with that 'ole dusty butt tonight?"

"What 'ole dusty butt?"

"People in the streets talk, Frank. I know you layin' up with that prostitute and if you think I can't tell when you're back on dope, then you must be crazy."

"You just dumb to the facts, baby. If you don't know what you talkin' 'bout, you'se better off not sayin' nothin'... I wouldn't mislead you, baby. I don't need to."

I knew she didn't believe me by the way her eyebrows were bunched together, her upper lip was curled, and her whole body was tight. I hadn't made love to her in awhile and I know that was the number one sign. When I had sex with Liz, I had to play it safe

Niyah Moore

because of her occupation. The fact that she was a hooker didn't bother me, but there was no way I was going to bring syphilis back to Carra Mae. Thankfully, Liz never gave me anything, but I was going to make sure. The time Liz and I spent together was mostly about getting high. Sex just came with it.

I tried to kiss Carra Mae's lips, but she stepped back, so I placed a kiss on my son's forehead as he slept in her arms. "I'll see you later, sweetheart. I have to get down to this club."

"I..." Tears were in her eyes as she put our son in the crib to sleep. "I know everything, Frank. Why do you think you can keep hiding stuff from me? Boy, if I didn't have this baby and the other one growin' inside me, I would leave you."

I stepped into her space, real close, stared into her eyes, and said, "You love me too much to leave me. The bills are paid 'round here and I'm takin' good care of you. So what if I get a lil' high from time to time... That doesn't mean I don't love you, baby." I tried to kiss her again, but she yanked away.

"Get outta my face with that crap, Frank."

I grabbed her as hard as I could and planted a moist kiss on her cheek. "I love you and I'll see you later on. I'll be home early."

She knew that was another lie as she stared through narrowed eyes, piercing my heart. She blocked the door, folding her arms across her chest.

"Carra Mae, don't start nothin' with me right now. You know I have to get to the club on time."

"Since when do you care about gettin' to the club on time? I've worked at the Champagne Supper Club and you've never been on time! We really need to talk and you're not leavin' here 'til I feel like I can trust you."

MAJOR JAZZ

"If you don't trust me then you just don't trust me. Now, get from in front of the door."

"No! I won't!"

I sat my things down and stared at her real hard. My patience had grown thin with her in a matter of seconds. Her hormonal ass was overreacting as usual. "Are you tellin' me that I'm gonna have to remove you myself?"

She scowled, twisting her angelic face into a frown. "How you think you're gonna do that, Frank?"

"Think about it. I'm a man, baby."

"I'm not movin' from in front of this door! I don't care if your ass is late! And if you think I'm gonna let you see that 'ole dusty butt again then you have another thing comin'. You listen to me real good... I'll beat your head as flat as a dime."

With a simple sweep, I lifted her off her feet and planted her on the couch. She stood up swiftly, reached on her tiptoes, and slapped me so hard I saw little birdies swirling around my head just like in the cartoons.

Out of reaction, I backhanded her across her face to see how she liked it. "Don't ever do that again, you hear me?" I picked up my things and walked out the door.

She cried, holding onto her face while screaming after me, "Come back here, Frank... Frank... Frank!"

I kept walking with my horn and sheet music ready to get the night started. Her loud sobbing made my stomach swirl, but I kept on with my stride. My right hand stung just like the right side of her face. I never thought I would hit her. Why did she have to push me that far? Shaking off the fucked up mood, I got into my car.

I played at the Champagne Supper Club and then headed on over to the Blue Mirror straight after. There was no way I was going back home just to argue with Carra Mae. Liz satisfied a few men and was done by the time I got there. As soon as I arrived, she handed me her money and cuddled up next to me at a booth. Rounds of drinks on the house, compliments of Miss Leola, started flowing and for that I owed her a song or two. I wasn't in the mood that night to play another note, but she accepted my rain check. Johnnie was out of jail after doing a few days, so the plan was to party all night long because he had the junk.

"Have another drink, Johnnie," I said.

Johnnie replied, "Thanks. You have no idea how happy I am to be out the clinker. I thought they were gonna keep me in there much longer. Now, I just have to find a way to keep my wife happy and my ass out of jail." He passed a reefer cigarette my way.

"Lucille ain't happy?" I puffed on it.

"All she wants to do is argue. I think she's pregnant and just don't want to tell me."

"Well, if you think she's pregnant, then she must be. Pregnant women become different women. They cry over every damned thing."

"She keeps tellin' her sisters she ain't, but she's packin' on some pounds."

"I saw her the other day and she has gained alotta weight. You asked her?"

"I've been too afraid to ask."

I laughed at him, passing the reefer back to him, and he joined my laughter.

"She's your wife, Johnnie. What would be so wrong if she got pregnant?"

"I didn't say anything was wrong with it. I'm just not ready to be a father."

MAJOR JAZZ

"I enjoy being a father. I just can't believe I'm 'bout to have baby number two. Our house is going to be a little hectic, I believe."

"So, y'all just a regular baby making factory over there?"

I nodded my head. "Looks that way."

Liz said closely against my ear, "What time we getting out of here? I need a fix."

"You can hold off, can't you, baby? I want to finish this drink first."

"How long that gonna take?"

"Not long, baby. You know I'm worth the wait."

"I sure do, Daddy." She smiled at me.

My low eyes went back to Johnnie as he drank. Liz's shaking hands had found their way into my lap. I could feel her nerves twitching. It was time for her to get a fix before her body got to trembling too badly. Her bottom lip quivered as if she were cold.

Just when I gulped the drink to prepare for us to leave, I noticed that Carra Mae had been standing on the other side of the bar, watching us. She had been a spectator of my infidelity. I was caught red handed. I froze. I didn't know how long she had been standing there or how much she actually witnessed. My gaze held hers.

My thought process on what to do next was delayed and maybe it was because I was truly too intoxicated to make sense out of what was happening. I loved Carra Mae and I didn't want her to be hurt by any of my wrongdoings, but the fire in her eyes told me I had hurt her soul beyond the normal threshold of pain.

I slowly lowered my arm from around Liz.

Liz looked up at me with a slight frown. "What's the matter, Blue?" Her eyes went in the direction I was staring and she, too, saw Carra Mae.

Niyah Moore

She had never seen Carra Mae before, but she could tell by the look on my face that she was my woman. Liz wrapped her lips around her drink and tried to act cool, but her nerves had the glass shaking.

Carra Mae walked on over, calmly with angered tears sliding down her face. Without words, she revealed a jackknife that she had tucked under her sleeve, and with one sharp swift movement, she went for Liz's neck. Liz put her hand up to block, but wound up getting stabbed through her hand.

I jumped up, knocking the table over, to stop Carra Mae from stabbing her again, but it was too late. She was a stabbing fool. Three, four, five times, Liz's piercing cry had the whole club in an uproar. I swept up the very pregnant Carra Mae, knocking the knife out of her hand, and carried her out of the club with her kicking and bucking to get free.

"Take her home before the wagon come," I said to Johnnie, carrying Carra Mae to his car.

"Put me down you low life bastard! I hate you, Frank! I hate you! I shoulda cut your ass instead! I hope that bitch dies!"

Johnnie unlocked his vehicle and I put her in his backseat. I didn't close the door until Johnnie had that thing started up. As soon as I closed the door, he sped off. I hurried back into the club and Miss Leola was wrapping Liz with cloths to keep the bleeding down. Liz was shaking and moaning. The amount of blood pouring from her had everyone afraid that she was going to die right there on the floor. Within thirty minutes, an ambulance had arrived. I rode with Liz to the hospital, holding her hand the entire time.

It was my fault. Guilt set in like a motherfucker. I had made Carra Mae a deranged crazy woman and my whore was bleeding to death. If I would've gone straight home after the gig, she wouldn't have had to come see about me to prove herself to be right.

The morphine they gave Liz helped her to cope with not getting the smack she craved. Thankfully, the doctor confirmed that her wounds weren't deep enough to cause any internal bleeding and no major arteries had been punctured. She was going to be fine. When the police came to ask some questions, she told them she didn't know who had done it. There were no witnesses that wanted to come forward, so the police's questions were pointless.

The police left and I had her hand still in mine. "Everything is gonna be alright, Liz."

She replied calmly, too drugged up to really talk, "Go home, Blue."

I knew there was no real future between us, so there was no need for me to blow my top. She turned her back to me, faced the window, and wept.

I left quietly. When I got back home, Carra Mae had packed up my son, some of their belongings, and left. The only thing she left was the shirt she was wearing that had specks of Liz's blood on it. My shame wouldn't let me go to her sister's house to bring them back. I figured if she wanted to be bothered with me, she would come home. The plan was to grovel on my knees and plead for her forgiveness, but I was as stubborn as an 'ole mule.

Frank

For weeks, I got high, night after night. I hardly slept, was running out of money, and was buskin' in the streets for my next fix. Without Carra Mae and my son, my life felt empty. My mother was getting sicker by the day and Cancer was taking its toll in her final stages. That's when Major came pounding on my door to help me get my life back on track. I checked into the treatment center like he asked me to and he whisked me off to New York.

I wrote Carra Mae letters once I got settled in. After a few months, she finally wrote me back with some short words. She told me that on the night my daughter was born, my mother lost her battle to Cancer. A life was gone, but a new one had arrived. She decided to name her Estelle in honor of my mother.

Coping with the untimely death of my mother, honestly, I was down and feeling real low, but not low enough to go back to using junk. I wanted to win Carra Mae back and the only way to do that was to stay clean. I flew back to San Francisco for my mother's funeral and had planned to leave as soon as it was over. I said a few words to my step-father and hugged my brother. Carra Mae and my babies were there. I hugged and kissed them too. My daughter was beautiful; she looked just like Carra Mae with the same ebony skin. I couldn't get enough of kissing on her. It was love at first sight for certain.

"Are you coming back with me?" I asked Carra Mae.

"No," she replied, turning away from my sober eyes.

As badly as that stung, I kissed them goodbye and hopped on the next flight.

Major and I kept recording in the studio and had gigs lined up with little to no effort, sometimes two in one night, to keep the both of us busy and relevant. I made plans to send for Carra Mae and the children, but she was hesitant about raising a family in New York. I didn't want to go back to the filthy 'Mo, not with all the tearing down they were doing to the buildings 'cause of that redevelopment mess they had going on. I heard the 'Mo wasn't going to be the same 'Mo we all loved. So, there was no need to go back.

"Why don't you and the babies come on? I have a nice apartment in Harlem and its enough room for all of us," I said to Carra Mae over the phone.

"What makes that place so different? Isn't that where you first started usin' that junk? Look, I can't take any more of your games, Frank. We have two beautiful children and I want to get married someday. I won't let you keep hurtin' me."

"I promise to marry you if you let me. I'm not usin' or abusin' anything again. I just take things one day at a time. That's all I can do. Each day, I'm growin' stronger. Please, baby, give me another chance. Please. I won't fuck up anymore. I need you."

"…Okay…"

My ears perked up. "You will?"

"Yes, I will, but you have to promise to do right by me and if you mess me over one more time, I'm gone for good, Frank."

"Right on… Oh, baby, you just made me the happiest man on the earth. I love you."

"I love you too, Frank."

Niyah Moore

I made sure our place was as perfect as possible with the money I made from gigging and recording. We had enough to live comfortably. I stayed away from everything that wasn't good for me including liquor. We had a fresh start in Harlem.

Major and I had just landed a gig at the Savoy. After the show, we were goofing around backstage. He had eased back into drinking hooch, but I didn't blast him for it. I remained clean 'cause Jazz was different sober and it felt good.

"I'm goin' back to the 'Mo," Major proclaimed.

I frowned. "Why? You've been gone for three years."

"Shit, I'm homesick. I need to see my mama... I really just miss being in the 'Mo. You don't think 'bout goin' back?"

I shook my head, but I understood where he was coming from. "If my mama was still alive, I would go back just for her, but I have too many bad memories 'bout that place. My life, here in Harlem, is just starting to be first-class."

"That's very true for you. Your family is on their way and you're smack free. I was born here, but it doesn't feel like home. Fillmo' will always be my home."

"I can dig it. You ever talk to Sallie?"

He shook his head. "I haven't talked to her since we left."

There was a knock on the dressing room door.

"Come in," I said.

A tall man with roasted coffee bean colored skin entered the dressing room. One look at him and I knew exactly who he was. It was like staring at my own face in the mirror. Major wore a confused look. He knew I didn't know my father and all the deep things I felt

MAJOR JAZZ

about the man I didn't know. How did he find me? With salt and peppered gray hair on his head, he didn't look as old as I thought he would look. Matter of fact, he looked pretty damned good for his age.

I wanted to speak first, but was unsure of what to say.

Major asked, "Can we help you, sir?"

He cleared his throat and removed his brim hat. "My name is Roy Frank Blue..."

Silence fell on the room and suddenly my palms got cold and sweaty. With a deep scowl on my face, I wasn't quite sure if I believed him. He looked like me, but how could I be so sure that he was my father?

"Estelle wrote me a letter before she died and expressed she wanted me to be a part of your life. That was her one dying wish and I would've fulfilled her wish sooner, only I thought you were in San Francisco..."

"My mother wrote you a letter?" My eyes scanned his, looking for a sign that would tell me he was making the whole thing up.

"Yeah. You're a hard man to catch up with. I spoke to Carra Mae over the phone a few days ago and she gave me the information regarding your show tonight." As tears escaped his eyes, tears welled up in mine. "I didn't want to miss it."

Carra Mae failed to mention that my father was looking for me. She didn't know how I was going to react, so she figured if she didn't tell me he was coming, I wouldn't have a way to avoid seeing him.

"I'll be outside if you need me." Major excused himself and left me to talk the man in private.

I stood up and looked the man square in the eyes. There were so many questions I had bottled up, but I didn't know where to begin. If my mother knew where he had been all that time, how come she kept him from me? *What was the truth?* I swallowed the hard forming lump in my throat as I stood just as tall as him. It was such a trip at how much we looked alike… even our heights were identical. I bet that was something my mother had trouble dealing with, but she never said things like, "You look just like your father," or anything like that, so who knows what was going on in her mind.

"Wow, she always would tell me how much you look just like me. I'm over here lookin' at you and it feels like I'm lookin' at the young me. Ain't that somethin'?" He chuckled.

"She kept in contact with you?"

He frowned at me as if he wasn't sure how come I didn't know. "Yeah… She always wrote and told me everything about you and your music. I couldn't be any happier to know you play the trumpet like me…"

My heart thumped rhythmically, produced a reverberating sound that only I could hear. "She never told me anything 'bout you."

"Is that so?"

"That's so. How come you weren't around?"

"I met your mother when she was only fourteen and it was love at first sight. I was nineteen, just drafted into the service. She got pregnant quick. My duty station had just reported me to Germany. I wanted to take her with me and marry her to make an honest woman out of her. She deserved that much, but her parents, your grandparents, wouldn't allow it. They actually wanted her to get an abortion, but she kept you. I made numerous attempts to send for her, but they all failed. So, I married another and started a family. That ripped your mother to shreds. She vowed to keep you away from me because she was hurt. I sent money every single month and made sure you always had a place to stay. When she got married, I still kept sending money because you were my responsibility. Eventually, my family and I made our home in Chicago. That's where we all live now."

I processed everything he said and though it was my first time hearing his version of the story, I felt a sense of relief to know he didn't just abandon me. I was silent and tears escaped my eyes. I wanted to blow my top, but I wasn't going to come undone. My mother deserved to rest in peace and I had to swallow the decision she made.

He continued, "You have four sisters, a host of nieces and nephews, and they all want to meet you. All their lives, they've known all about you."

"Forgive me if I don't know what to say. This is very overwhelming."

"That's understandable. I'm just glad to see you're doing well. Your mother told me about... about your addiction... and she thought she was going to lose you. Hearing her cry on the phone to me, I knew I had to see you before... We prayed so hard." He broke down and cried.

I hugged him. As hard as I tried to fight the tears that seemed to be caught in my chest and throat, it was no use. We were both crying. Their prayers saved my life. My own prayers had been answered that day because I finally got to meet my father. That was one of the happiest days of my life... a pivotal turn of events... and though I never went back to live in the 'Mo, I was glad to be part of such a happenin' time. Memories, good, bad, whatever... I will never forget that place.

Major Jazz

"What we play is life." – Louis Armstrong

Fillmore was like Harlem on the bay. Sammy Davis Jr., Ella Fitzgerald, Dinah Washington, and Duke Ellington all fell into San Francisco the way they had in the Big Red Apple. It was the closest thing to Harlem with nicer weather…the reason why my parents loved it so much. When I was two years old, we left Harlem. Fillmore became our new beloved home. The saying, *There's no place like home,* held true for me. I've traveled the world and still to this day, I feel the same love for the 'Mo. The city was tough, but happenin'. There were plenty of gigs to go around for anyone and everyone who had an instrument to play. MUSIC WAS ALIVE. That's what I loved most.

My mother was classically trained to sing Opera. She was quite the loving mother, wife of a jazz musician, Jamaican raised in Queens, and the sweetest, darkest woman I had ever known. After I was born, she got real sick with an unknown disease. Docs weren't able to save her reproductive system, so I was the only child. I heard her blame Pop once for the disease, once and once only. No more talks of that nonsense was allowed because Pop's insulting words were constantly followed by powerful blows from his big fists.

I was too young to understand the dynamics of their abusive, dysfunctional marriage, but when I got old enough, I understood fully that Pop was an abusive, half Jewish, green-eyed bastard child from Brooklyn, bottom line, and pretended not to know any better. To say he was the perfect husband would be a lie. His infidelities weren't a secret and he blamed moonshine every single time my mama's accusations flew out of her mouth like darts. Dodging them as if he were fighting for his life, his drunken stupor always led to Mama balling herself up in the corner, using her back to protect her from his punches and kicks.

When things were bad, they were bad. Food, milk, and clothes were a struggle whenever he was in between gigs. My mother did her absolute best to keep our tea kettle full of eggs and homemade preserves stocked. Our Japanese neighbor, Suk, got us through with whatever she could help with and gave us lots of rice.

Getting a real job, to Pop, was something he frowned upon. Music was the only job he was going to work. Mama wanted to go back to singing to help out on the bills, but he was against it because he was the man. No woman of his was going to support our family. She tried to secretly get a gig, but that ended as soon as she started. He dragged her out of that club by her hair in front of everybody. The beatings were more frequent when we didn't have money, so she couldn't win for losing.

"Bitch, I'll kill you," he had said on that night with his hands around her throat so tight she was turning blue.

I jumped on his back to protect her. "Get off her! Pop, you're gonna kill her!"

He snapped out of it as if he didn't realize that his own strength could actually end her life. With the release of her limp body, he shouted at the top of his lungs, "Next time, you do what I tell you!" He slammed the door on his way out, causing Mama's pictures to fall off the wall.

I try not to think about the bad times because Pop was a hell of a drunk on bootlegged, white whiskey. There were good times. Whenever he came home with a big smile, a few bags full of chicken, bacon, pork chops from the butcher, and some fish for Mama to fry, we knew money was going to be around for a little while and he was going to be in the best mood. On those good days, my parents made love heavily... so loudly, a pillow couldn't protect my ears from my mama's rising sex sounds. "Yes! Yes! Albert!" Even though I couldn't stand that sound either, I preferred it over the beatings any day.

1355 Buchanan Street was where we lived. That's where all of my memories, good and bad, happened. Mama had these specialty dishes that she liked to cook. Everyone adored her coconut cakes and rum punch -- recipes straight from Jamaica -- traditions handed down from her mother and her mother's mother. My favorite was her fried plantains with rice and chick peas. Mmmmm. Yummy.

When Pop wasn't fighting my mother, he was out late, all night even, sleeping with a host of other women after gigs. I mean, she would cheat, too. I remember being in my room with my twelve year-old cousin, my babysitter, who was an elementary school dropout.

Whenever Mama said, "Stay in your room, Cricket, 'til I tell you to come out," I knew the deal.

Mama was pantin' and sweatin' on top of the next man in the front room. My cousin would turn up a record to drown out her sounds. Mama had her own needs and needed to feel some sort of love.

MAJOR JAZZ

Major Ingram was the name I was blessed with because my daddy loved to play songs on the C Major scale, but my mama called me Cricket, a nickname she adored. She said I chirped like a cricket as a baby, a loud irksome sound, yet it was beautiful. She explained that when crickets chirped a calling song that they attracted females and repelled other males. Every time I chirped loudly, women always came to coo me. From birth, I had a special calling song that entranced women by the dozens… seemed like anyway.

Pop taught me everything he knew about jazz, which was a whole lot. He could play the trumpet, piano, sax, drums and bass, but he played the sax with much more passion. He was naturally gifted to play by ear and couldn't read notes worth a damn. Since he refused to go to musician's school to learn to read music, he got better at picking up any song and playing it as he heard it. He spoon fed me the blues from the first day I opened my eyes to the world. By the time I was eleven, I could play everything he could play, only better 'cause I could read it. I had even mastered his solos.

I played with no clams and made no mistakes.

He bought a used piano and it crowded our living room amongst all the other instruments he had. We played together almost every day if he was in the mood and Mama would sing her heart out.

Sometimes, people would come by for dinner parties and we would entertain them. Mama would cook dinners and we would give our company quite a show, song after song, well past into the wee hours. We always kept our windows opened. Our neighbors would open their windows and enjoy our sounds from their houses.

Niyah Moore

"Whew, that canary 'sho can chirp!" Pop shouted, sweating before blowing into that sax sweetly.

With a head nod I agreed, playing those keys, following his lead.

My mother had one of the most incredible ranges and could sing eight octaves effortlessly. It was a shame that she could no longer sing on a stage because of Pop's jealousy. He always thought she wanted to sing to cheat on him, but she didn't need to sing to do that. I always hoped she would go back to singing, but she never did. Around the house while she cleaned was the best time to hear her sing. She gave me Goosebumps when she hit those operatic high ranges.

I took lessons on Sutter to learn how to read music ever since I was little. Classical taught me elegance and poise, but bebop became a favorite of mine. I remember sneaking down to the most happenin' spot, Bop City. I couldn't have been any older than sixteen. I hopped on that itty bitty stage at the back of the room without any fear and challenged the house pianist. My improvised solos were something I worked real hard on. My most challenging critic was Pop. I already knew that if he was impressed, I could impress anybody. The tough crowd didn't dare wave me off as I proved to be much better than the house pianist.

Jim, the owner of Bop City, fired the house pianist and gave me a regular gig making fifty dollars a week on the spot. Late nights, musicians sat around in there talking about chords, putting music together, and anything musical period. It was a musician's sanctuary. The jam sessions that went on in there, whew, you had to be there to see it - mind blowing. Thursday nights was called Celebrity Night and I had the opportunity to meet every famous person that ever stepped foot in there. The parties would go on nonstop until six in the morning. That's when everyone went home. The streetcars and buses went everywhere in the city and ran all night, so transportation was never a problem.

I tried to hide the gig at Bop City for as long as I could from my parents, but with the way the whole neighborhood had started spreading it around, it wasn't long before word got back to Mama.

"That Major, you know Margery and Albert's boy? He 'sho can jig. He's been playin' down at Bop City. You gotta get down there and hear him. He's *shaaaaaaarp*."

Mama talked amongst her friends, "How can a place, like that, let a child inside? Cricket is just a baby."

No one could give her the answer because they didn't know how I was allowed to be on that stage at that time of night. It wasn't like I was playing worry free. I kept my eyes on the door just in case Pop came up in there.

Jim was downright pissed off that I had snuck my ass in there to play underage, but I was so good, he just went on ahead and let me slide. "Now, look here, Major. I'm gonna go 'head and let you still play, but if the cops come up in here, you better take your ass out the back door."

I didn't have any problem with that. "You got it, Jim."

That was made clear.

When I got home that night, I crept through the window, and Mama was sitting on my bed in the dark. She turned on the light with a deep scowl and her bottom lip was pursed together tight with a belt in her hand. I knew that look all too well. I swallowed hard and prepared myself for the whooping I was about to get. I drew in a deep breath, stood up straight, and started explaining, "Mama…"

She held up her hand, letting me know to save my breath. "What you doing out at this time of night?"

"I was at Bop City."

"What you doing down there?"

I paused to think of a lie.

"Answer me," she demanded.

"…I have a gig there five nights a week."

"What 'bout school?"

"I still get up and go... My grades are real good. I never sleep much anyway, even when I don't play over there."

Her shoulders dropped as she sat on the bed. As she took in air and blew it back out, she patted a spot next to her. I sat. "I know you love playin', Cricket. I just hope your father don't find out…" Her voice trailed off as it trembled a bit.

"I plan on tellin' him, Mama."

"Good. When?"

"Tomorrow."

"You makin' good money over at the house that bop built?"

I stood up, went over to my top drawer, took out the jar full of money, a few hundred dollars, reached into my pocket to get the money I made that night, and I tried to give it to her.

She smiled at me, placing her hand on mine. "Cricket, you worked hard for your money. You keep saving it."

I went ahead and took fifty dollars; a week's pay, and gave it to her anyway. "Buy you somethin' nice for once. You deserve it, Mama."

After kissing me on the cheek, she tucked the money away in her bra, and left me alone to go to sleep.

MAJOR JAZZ

I didn't get around to actually telling Pop about the gig the next day or the day after because every time I thought of telling him, my fear deterred me. He was going to beat my tail black and blue without a question, so I prolonged it for as long as I could.

He was at Bop City one night and I had gotten word. He was looking for me, so I tiptoed out the back. Someone must've told him I had just left because he came home madder than he was when he sought out to find me in the first place.

Mama had just finished cooking fried fish and bammy, something she hadn't made in a long time. He slammed the door as soon as he was in. "Major!"

Pop took one look at the food and knew he hadn't brought home money in a while. He hadn't noticed, but we had been eating well for weeks without him. He hadn't been home because he had been at another woman's pad, shacking up over there.

I was at the table about to eat as if I had been there the whole night.

Pop's nostrils flared and then he knocked the whole meal onto the hardwood floor. "You think you'se a better man than me? You ain't shit! You don't have what it takes to be better than me!"

POW... I was next.

The blow from the back of his hand was too powerful and drew blood. As much as my own anger flared inside, I didn't dare fight him back with my hands. He was wrong... I was already better than him. My steady gig was my way of fighting back. I always had bread and I provided for us. Bread had a way of finding me even when I didn't need it. If he hadn't been such a drunk, he would've been able to keep his gigs. He only had himself to blame.

Niyah Moore

"Now clean up this fuckin' mess! Major, don't leave this house no more tonight!"

He stormed out of the house, slamming the door causing the pictures to fall.

I held onto my bleeding mouth as Mama rushed for a cold towel. I was tired of his abuse and wondered if she was too. I could see the hurt in her teary eyes, but she was helpless, and that's when I noticed a bruise was forming around her left eye. He beat her before he came looking for me at Bop City. We exchanged our pained silence before she cleaned up the mess he had made.

As I rolled my tongue around in my mouth, I realized Pop had knocked out my corner tooth on the right side of my mouth. That's how I ended up with a gold tooth in its place.

I tried to fight my infuriated tears. My heart hardened and formed a thick layer of protection. No one would be able to hurt me the way he had.

Mama tried to soothe the lingering after burn as she said, "Don't worry about dinner, Cricket. I have some more I can make."

"I'm not hungry, Mama." I sniffled, wiping my mouth.

My boys, Tyrone and Tyrell, came knocking on the door to see if I was going to go back to Bop City.

Mama answered, "He's staying in tonight, boys. He'll see you tomorrow."

They were my running buddies since we were kids. Tyrone was a jamming drummer and Tyrell was a cold saxophone player. We formed our own band once we met Frank Blue at Bop City. He was something else on that trumpet. Junk tried to lay a heavy toll on his jazz, but man oh man, we were on fire when we got together. As soon as we all graduated from high school, we joined the Musician's Union, and played all night long every night. The sun greeted us and that was our signal for us to go home. By the time I turned twenty, I was considered one of the best paid pianists in the 'Mo.

I was too dedicated to my music... real gone with the ivory and ebony keys to really stay with one woman. My first love was a Japanese girl named Hiromi. Beauty beyond my eyes was what I had gained as a prize. That's how mixed up our neighborhood was. We hung out with our friends, Japanese, Black, Jewish, and Filipino at the theater to watch old cowboy flicks. We kissed once. Our love was short lived because during WWII, the Japanese that once occupied the neighborhood had to go to Japanese Camps. It was like overnight all of the Japanese families that lived in the Western Addition left. It was strange not seeing her or even our neighbors. Places like Yu Zen's Bakery became Dee's Chicken Shack. You get the picture? All of their homes became occupied by black people who migrated from the south. Heartbroken, I vowed to never let a girl get that close to my heart again. I remember crying for a whole week.

"Cricket, put your tears into your music. Play whatever you feel whenever you feel it." Mama had a way with words that worked with me.

My love for piano intensified through my struggle to get over Hiromi. Of course in my adult life I had my share of plenty beautiful women to keep me company, but my desire never lasted long enough to make any one of them my one and only back then.

I dated Sallie Aquino for a while. Her eyes reminded me of Hiromi's. That was the first thing I noticed. Boy was she beautiful, a drop dead beauty with style, and a hell of a lover. She had one of the greatest strengths like a tree with mightiness and power. She exuded an aura of coolness and spread a fragrance that was inviting.

"What's your tale, nightingale?" she asked the very first time we met at Bop City.

I knew I had to have her as I inched towards her.

I could feel the wave of chills that entered her body while my lips grazed the tip of her earlobe when I replied, "My name is Major. What's yours?"

Her natural train of thought had been interrupted; I could tell as she answered, "It's a pleasure to finally meet you personally, Major." She cleared her throat. "My name is Sallie."

"It's my pleasure to meet you as well, Sallie."

"What's a smooth lookin' cat like you doin' down here at this time of the morning?"

It was near three in the morning, but I couldn't sleep until the music inside of me hibernated. I could never sleep well while my mind ran like a mad man without a regulator and that made it hard for me to sleep at all.

As much as I wanted to chat with her, it was time for me to get on that stage, so I was going to have to talk to her at another time. "I'm the man everyone is here to see. Excuse me."

"Later alligator…"

"After while crocodile…"

She watched me do my thing and couldn't get enough. She kept showing up at Bop City with her two sisters, Lucille and Sade. Night after night, she waited for me to come to her. Most nights, she would be wearing those dresses so fine, just the way God made her, and it was like some unknown magnetic force drew me to her. Taking her home with me was something she wanted just as bad as I did.

MAJOR JAZZ

Ginger Robinson... shit, our heated passion created some of my best compositions, but I was cursed with my daddy's blood. I knew better than to get into a commitment with her. Some nights Ginger would come up to the club and then back to my place. She had flowing, reddish brown hair, tiny freckles on her nose, full lips, and deep brown eyes. Though our relationship became tougher when our child was stillborn, somehow we managed to mend our broken spirits. We both agreed on not ever getting together because we were like oil and water; we just didn't mix. Sexually, we were like a stick of dynamite... once lit there was no way to stop an explosion from happening. All we could do was duck for cover.

Ginger gasped as she tried to find the breath I took from her each time my tongue licked her. I pleased her with my mouth between her thighs. I didn't please all women that way - just her. She carried my child and that thought alone made her sexy.

"I want to have another baby," she uttered between moans.

I, too, longed to have another child, one that would live and breathe, but maybe it was to only replace the sadness I felt for losing the first one. I couldn't tell which, but I didn't really want to make another baby with her. If it was meant to be, then it would be I figured, but I wasn't going to force it. It wouldn't have been fair to leave her to raise our child alone, especially not when my desire for seeing other women was so prevalent.

"Shhhh," I hushed her, bringing my lips up to her breasts.

I sucked.

She moaned.

I sucked some more.

Niyah Moore

She screamed for me…

We sexed in the light of the moon between of the iridescent sheets, and moments later, we realized we couldn't stand to be in the same room. Too many memories of what we lost and our pain was something that took too long to get over. Pain revisited seemed to hurt more than pain first inflicted. We commenced to easing into one another's beds whenever it suited us, but she wanted me to belong to only her.

I just couldn't.

When Pop was murdered by a man for messing around with that man's woman, it broke my mother's heart for years. It took her months just to get out of the bed. A part of me was glad he wasn't around anymore to hurt her, but then another part of me missed hearing him playing his saxophone in the morning. I didn't want to hurt any woman the same way my father had hurt my mother. As much as I heard my mama's cries when I was younger, there was just no other way with me. Love was going to have to wait.

There was only one *her*… jazz music.

Major

"Music is my mistress and she plays second fiddle to no one." – Duke Ellington

My perfectly tuned baby grand piano sat in the middle of my living room. I paid a pretty penny for it. One of my most prized possessions and I didn't care 'cause it was all mine. In the one bedroom sublet apartment I rented, it took up most of the floor. While a lit Camel cigarette perched on the very edge of my lips, I let my fingers caress the keys of the piano the same way I caressed a supple woman's body, slowly and with a great deal of skill. As I pressed chords, the felt-covered hammer struck the steel strings to produce a pretty sound. The hammers rebounded, allowing the strings to continue vibrating at their resonant frequency as the melody progressed. Those vibrations sent a sweet sensation from the floorboards straight up to my spine and were transmitted through the bridge to the sounding board that coupled the acoustic energy out into the air. When I released the keys, a damper stopped the string's vibrations. The harder I pressed the keys, the louder the sound became. The greater the velocity, the greater the force of the hammer hit the strings, and the louder the note became, much like a woman climaxing during sex.

She cried my name, "Major! Major!"

I closed my eyes and listened to her intently, knowing just how I wanted to play her. The way her melody just lingered, nothing on earth was like her love for me. My love for her was unconditional.

I stopped abruptly, inhaled the smoke from my cigarette, flicked the ashes into the ashtray, wiped the sweat from my forehead with the back of my hand, and gulped gin from a glass on the piano. I thought I would never drink, especially because of Pop, but it helped to take the pressure off my busy mind. After a long night of jamming until morning, I slept all afternoon, and then got up to jam all over again, drinking throughout the whole day.

Most women didn't hang around long enough to compete with the piano for my time and affection. Sallie, on the other hand, had the persistence of a salesman. On her first visit, I stared at Sallie for a moment from my piano as she tidied up my apartment. She washed dishes, swept, and mopped with Mr. Clean like she really enjoyed doing it for me. I guess that was her way of showing she could take care of me if the chance ever arose. Her Asian looking eyes were warm after she cleaned up and I felt weird all of a sudden. I wasn't so sure if I really wanted a romance to blossom between us, but it was blossoming beyond my control.

Sallie came over to me once she tossed the dishrag in the sink. "So, this is where all the magic happens..."

"Most of it anyway... I create tunes any place where there's a piano... Do you recognize this tune?"

"It sounds familiar."

"I played this the other night at Bop City."

"Oh yes..."

I sung the chorus for her and she looked surprised that I could hold a tune.

"You have a nice singing voice."

"Thank you. I get that from my mother." My fingers continued to move gracefully across the black and white keys.

Niyah Moore

"How come you don't sing while you play at the clubs?"

"I leave the singing to the singers. Speaking of singers, you know the young lady that was at Bop City last night?"

She nodded, "Yes."

"Do you think you can help me out with her? You know, like her style and whatnot?"

Her grin spread. "I would love to help you."

Before switching the melody, I gently pulled her hand to sit on my lap. She straddled me, to my surprise, and placed her arms around my neck. I wasn't expecting her to be so sensual. I thought she would sit to the side with her legs closed. Needless to say, I was aroused by the heat that was coming from between her legs. I played another sweet song, slower than the last, keeping my hazel eyes on hers while inching my way closer to her face until my lips landed. We kissed with so much passion that I stopped playing. My hands finally found their way up her dress. She moaned as my tongue moved easily in and out of her mouth. Our tongues danced so sweetly, mimicking the melody I played.

We parted and stared at one another as we caught our lost breaths. The air we took in was now the exhalation from one another. Breathing in unison, we created a rapport and stimulated more excitement. A look of confusion came across my face as I swallowed hard. "What you tryin' to do to me, Sallie?"

"I'm tryin' to make you fall in love me."

The "L" word usually made my skin crawl, but the way she said it and the look in her eyes hypnotized me. I closed my eyes to come out of the trance I felt creeping amongst me. I wasn't sure what to call what we were doing, but I was falling just as fast and hard for her as she was for me. I opened my eyes to find that I couldn't take my eyes off her. "I think I may be falling in love with you," I uttered without thinking.

"But…"

"But?" She scrunched up her nose, making the cutest little face.

"Only time will tell…"

"Are you still in love with Ginger?"

"Why you ask me?"

"I heard through the grapevine that you're still seeing her."

"I care for her. Ginger and I have a connection no one will ever be able to understand. She was pregnant once… Our daughter passed away."

"I'm truly sorry that happened."

"It was painful for the both of us, but we're much better 'bout it now. Only God holds our fate. Are you lookin' to fall in love with me?"

"From the moment I first laid my eyes on you, I knew you would drive me crazy like this. One day I hope to be more than just your friend. Now that I finally have you in my arms, I don't want to let you go."

"So, don't let me go."

I felt the heat rise underneath my face and a huge grin appeared. I kissed her again, that time feeling her bare legs. She sucked my tongue while inhaling me. A wave of chills shot up my spine to the back of my neck. We kissed like long time lovers, familiar with one another's tongue strokes. I moaned with the anticipation of having her right there, on top of my piano. I wasn't making it easy for her to say no. That was the point. I didn't want her to tell me no.

She laughed as if she could read my polluted mind, gave me a quick peck before easing from my lap. "I better get goin'," she said, biting on her lower lip.

Niyah Moore

"Already?" I asked.

The look in her eyes changed a bit, became real sexy like as she pulled her dress down. She gathered her coat and purse. "It's really late. I don't want to walk home any later than now."

"I can give you a ride. I have somewhere to be in a little while anyway. I can just take you home on my way."

Sallie's eyes danced around with mine as if she could still hear the music coming out of my pores. "That's fine with me, but I don't want to mess up your plans. You have somewhere else to be and I'm sure you need to be there on time. I should go ahead and leave now."

I got to the door before her. "Don't leave. I want you to stay a little bit longer." Both of my hands went to her face as I kissed her again. She dropped her things at the door as if I was just too irresistible to resist. Pushing her body up against the door, I tasted her lips, chin, and neck, all while making her moan louder each time my lips converged her skin.

She said against my lips as if she suddenly remembered we had a small problem, "What about Ginger?"

"What about her?"

"I don't want to cause any problems."

"You won't." By then I had already started lifting up her dress.

Before I could get it completely over her head, there was a knock on the door. She quickly pulled it back down and ran her hand over her jet-black hair, stepping away from the door. "Are you expecting someone?"

MAJOR JAZZ

I closed my eyes and nodded. It had slipped my mind that fast. I wiped her lipstick from my lips and opened the door.

Tyrone walked in. "You ready, Major?"

"Yeah, I'm ready."

"Hey there, Sallie, it's good to see you."

"Hey, Tyrone, how are you doing?"

"I'm good. Are you coming along with us?"

I raised my eyebrow at her. Now that was a thought. If she came with us, then I could get her to spend the night with me. My eyes tended to have a way with her, so I used them to ask her to join us silently.

"Sure…" she replied.

"Grab your things and let's go. Billie Holiday is at the New Orleans Swing Club waiting for us. She thought you were coming down there to do a quick run through before, but I see you've been a little tied up…"

"Oh shit, yeah, I forgot 'bout that." Fooling around with Sallie and I forgot about my other obligations at the club.

"You know how she feels about switchin' up pianists at the last minute. She walked in cursin' and the first person she asked to see was you."

Lady Day always asked for me whenever she played in the 'Mo. I didn't mind playing for her, but I hated the way she would be slumped over singing at times. That junk was laying a toll on her singing and I hoped her depression would soon be over, so she could be well. Ever since she got busted for narcotics over at the Mark Twain Hotel downtown, she just hadn't been the same. She never talked about what troubled her, but she sure did show it in her performances.

"Alright, we're gonna head on over there right now," I replied.

Niyah Moore

The three of us got in my '51 Chevy Bel Air convertible top and went down to the New Orleans Swing Club. I was glad Sallie wanted to tag along. That was the first time of many times she came with me to my gigs.

When we got there, we couldn't find Lady Day. The club was filling up and our headliner was missing.

The club owner said, "Miss Holiday doesn't feel good and isn't going to perform tonight."

The club was nearly full and the house band was on stage. What did he mean she wasn't performing? "Come again," I asked.

"Lady Day is back in her hotel suite at the Manor Plaza Hotel with one of her little Chihuahuas keeping her company. She's not performing."

"You still want my band to play tonight?" I asked him.

"That would be just fine. Meet me after the show for your pay."

"Sweet."

Tyrone went outside to wait for the rest of the band to show up. I took Sallie's hand in mine.

"Thank you for inviting me with you guys, tonight," Sallie said.

"Thank you for coming along. Say, would you like somethin' to drink? Are you hungry?"

"I can go for a little somethin'."

"Sit right here in the front and I'll have someone bring you a lil' somethin'." I smiled at her before placing a kiss on her hand.

Soaking in all the affection I showed her, her smile spread the biggest I had ever seen it.

I walked over to the bar, ordered a hot turkey and Swiss on soft roll with a small salad. "Make sure the pretty lady up front gets that order. She's my special guest. Oh, and send her one of those specialty cocktails you got there."

"You got it, Major."

I winked and went outside to smoke for a minute before our set. Tyrell and Frank were getting out of Frank's car. To my surprise, Frank looked good that night. He didn't seem to be drugged up. That's how it was with Frank. One minute, he was sober. The next, he was loaded. He was too unpredictable.

"What's goin' on? Are we jookin' for Lady Day or what?" Tyrell questioned, reaching for one of my Camels.

I handed him one. "She's not feelin' too hot. Regardless, we're still playin'."

"You think Candy Cane can come down and sing?" Frank asked.

"No... She's got school in the morning."

Frank walked inside the club and Tyrone followed him. Tyrell and I finished smoking before going in. When the house band was done, we set up. As we played, we got through maybe one song before Lady Day walked onto the stage. Her eyes were so low that she looked sleepy. She didn't care if we weren't done with the song we were playing. She was feeling fine enough to sing, so she sang in the middle of the song without a care in the world. That's how she felt. The crowd whistled. Everyone was glad that Lady Day made it down to bless the place with her presence. It didn't matter if she only did half a song.

I looked over to where Sallie was sitting and she looked amazed. I wasn't sure if she ever saw Billie perform, but the look on her face told me she had not. Her awe made me smile and in the back of my mind, my thoughts were on pleasing her later.

Major

"Don't play what's there, play what's not there." – Miles Davis

I woke up to her kisses the next morning. It was early... around seven. For the first night in a long time, I slept more than five hours. In her arms, I felt a level of comfort that was missing from my life. The feel of her fingertips as she grazed my bare chest felt too good. We were alone... undisturbed without any music playing in the background... only in our hearts. I was grateful for the way she showed her affection and the lovemaking from the night before was mind blowing.

"Good morning, handsome," she sang.

"Good morning, beautiful."

"You want some coffee this morning?"

I frowned. I usually woke up to a glass of gin and a piece of toast. "No, thank you. Say, what you got planned tonight?"

"I don't have any plans yet."

"You feel like goin' out to the Champagne Supper Club for dinner? I don't have any gigs, but we may go on over to Bop City to see what's goin' on afterwards."

Sallie looked surprised that I would suggest doing something as intimate and private as dinner. I was in a good mood and I purposely didn't have a gig. I took the night off to spend some time with her.

"Sure, I'll go to dinner with you."

"Good. I'll pick you up around six thirty. How's that sound?"

"That sounds good to me."

My hands caressed her body. Sallie was petite, barely five feet tall, much like a Filipino woman, and weighed 115 pounds. I wafted over her neck and inhaled her faint touch of rose smelling fragrance, a remnant of what she sprayed on her body the previous morning. My mounting solidity wanted to be inside of her once again before she departed for the day.

Her hands, too, roamed, arousing me with her caress. I placed my lips back on hers as I positioned myself between her thighs, grabbing hold of her plump bottom. She opened up for me and I entered upon her invite. The deepest part of me wanted to make her mine for a lifetime. The other part of me on the surface was afraid my cursed blood would ruin us. I pushed every thought to the farthest place of my mind and moved in and out of her wetness.

Moaning in my ear, I helped her reach her climax quickly. Moments later, I reached mine. I loved to kiss her because she was good at it. I sucked on her top lip before getting out of bed to bathe. "You can stay around a little while longer if you like, but I have a recording session in a lil' bit."

"I have to get home." She sat up with her messy curly hair all over her head.

"Take your time, sweetheart." I grabbed my towel.

"I'll see you later?"

"Indeed you shall."

More kisses between us before she gracefully eased out of the bed with the white sheet still draped around her. I headed to the bathroom, feeling like I was drifting. The perfect melody for a love song hit me. Before I could get into the bathtub, I played it.

Niyah Moore

"I love you," Sallie uttered on her way out of the door.

I didn't hear her over my music.

***

I picked up Sallie around eight thirty. I was two hours late and hated that our first date was going to start off on the wrong foot, but the jam session ran a little longer than I expected it to because Blue was late. Whenever we ran on his clock, nothing got done on time. She didn't say a word when she answered the door, only wore a smile of relief, dressed in her Sunday's best.

"Well, don't you look beautiful?"

"Thank you. I almost thought you weren't comin'."

"I'm sorry I'm late," I said.

"Well, you're here now and I'm ready," she answered sweetly.

"Where y'all goin'?" Sade asked from behind her.

"Mind your business," Sallie snapped back.

"I am minding my own business. Where you takin' my sister, Major?"

I smiled at Sade. She was a bossy 'lil 'ole something and that sass of hers made her cute as a button. I didn't mind her asking questions. That was just her way. "I'm taking her to dinner at the Champagne Supper Club."

"Ooooh, fancy smancy…. Say, why don't you two join us at Club Flamingo later? We're goin' dancin' tonight."

"No," Sallie responded quickly. "We have other plans. Now, take your tail back in the house and leave me be."

"I can't stand you." Sade shut the door.

I chuckled. "Is she always that way?"

"Always." Sallie rolled her eyes.

I opened the door for her to get into the car, closed her in, and went around to the driver's side.

As I pulled away from the curb she said, "You look nice, tonight. Do you spend a lot of time in the mirror?"

I laughed. "Not too much outside of shaving. I don't groom for too long."

Sallie's eyes lit up like a Christmas tree. "Well, you always look so well put together in your tie, suspenders, and slacks. Your dress shirts are always so crisp. You press them yourself?"

"Thank you, darling. No, I take them to the cleaners over on Fillmore."

She beamed proudly. She knew her family's cleaners pressed my clothes.

"Would that be the Aquino's Cleaners you speak of?"

"That's right, only the best cleaners for fifty cents." I winked at her.

We arrived at the Champagne Supper Club and sat at our reserved table near the side of the stage. Frank and the house band were playing some good sounds. The Champagne Supper Club had so much class... real upscale. It wasn't the greasy chicken at the Chicken Shack or Waffle House. That place was first class dining at its finest. One of the cocktail waitresses came to our table to take our drink order. I ordered a bottle of champagne on ice, something I hadn't done in a while. I was trying to impress.

Niyah Moore

Sallie eyed the menu and I could tell she was stunned by the prices. We were going to spend some money that night.

"Order whatever you like."

"I don't know what I want. Hmmm…"

I observed her beauty and for a short while I imagined spending the rest of my life with her. I silently wondered what our children would look like if that day were to come. We both had some mixed up blood and the combination would be a sight to see.

"What do you suggest?"

"Try the Fillet Mignon. I believe it comes with rice pilaf and steamed vegetables," I said glancing over the menu.

"That sounds good. I think I'll go ahead and have that. Will you order for me? I have to go to the ladies room."

"No sweat."

When she got up to go to the bathroom, I couldn't help but stare at how amazing she looked in that dress. A wave of chills moved up and down my spine confirming just how lucky I was to have her.

Sallie went into the ladies room. After she got done using the stall, she washed her hands, and checked her face in the mirror. She re-applied a little more lipstick and dabbed her lips on a paper towel.

Ginger walked in and checked herself out in the mirror right next to her. Sallie immediately tensed up and stared at the tight fitting green glittery dress Ginger had on. A look of disgust plastered her face. She had come in Ginger's paths a few times too many whenever I was around, but that was the first time they were actually face to face and Sallie wasn't too thrilled about it.

MAJOR JAZZ

"What you doin' here?" Ginger asked, staring at Sallie as if she was beneath her.

"What? I don't have a right to be here or somethin'? You own the place?"

Ginger put her hands on her curvy hips. "I don't own the place. I'm just asking you a question."

"I'm havin' dinner just like you…"

"What you doin'? You havin' dinner with my man?"

"Who's your man?" Sallie retorted.

"You know who my man is… Major Ingram."

"You're such a silly heifer. He's not your man."

Ginger laughed, throwing her head back. "I was just in his bed the other night. There are so many things you have yet to learn when it comes to him. Major is all show and no go, honey. He can't get rid of me 'cause I'm not goin' anywhere. I'll always be his."

Usually, Sallie would've said something back just as nasty, but was too hurt by Ginger's words. She knew I was still seeing Ginger and Ginger knew I was seeing Sallie. Hell, why were they so upset? I didn't know what the fuss was about.

Instead of responding, Sallie stormed out of the bathroom and came back to our table with a big attitude. I was in the middle of ordering, so I didn't notice the look on Sallie's face until the waitress left the table.

"What's the matter?" I asked, observing the tiny tears that she was trying to hold back.

"I'm not gonna compete for your heart anymore. If you want to still see Ginger Robinson, then why don't you just be with her?"

I swallowed some champagne. I had already made up in my mind to choose Sallie, but I wasn't expecting a confrontation about it. I didn't like being confronted. My defense mechanism came in full swing as I gripped the champagne glass. Right before I could tell her like it was, Ginger strolled over to the table and placed her hand on her hip. Sallie brushed her tears away and sucked it up. She didn't want to appear as if her feathers had been ruffled.

"You know, I'm really gettin' sick of your same 'ole song and dance, Major," Ginger said. "I thought you said she was just gonna help you with that girl you done discovered. Now, your skillet is tryin' to promote a meal? It's over. I wouldn't give you any air if you were stopped up in a jug."

I didn't show Ginger any emotion. I sat there coolly. She had the nerve to talk to me that way when she was clearly there with another man. I saw her the moment we walked in. She had been flirting, laughing, and kissing on him. How could she talk about games when she was screwing around, too?

"What you want with this gator-faced broad?" She continued to badger.

Sallie bit her tongue and stared at me, waiting for me to defend her.

"Isn't that your date across the room, waitin' for you?" I nodded my head across the club.

"Yeah, and?" Ginger rolled her neck. "I keep waitin' 'round on you, I'll never be happy!"

"If your feet don't hurry up and take you 'way from here, you'll *ride* away."

Ginger stared me down as if that was supposed to mean shit to me. She didn't want to get me to jumping salty because that was never a good look for anybody. "You don't have to threaten me to get me to leave. Don't you call me anymore, Major. Dig me? What we have is through. I'm not puttin' out a thing."

MAJOR JAZZ

I saluted her like a soldier to send her on her way. She didn't even finish her dinner with her date. He was sitting there, wondering what the hell just happened as she left out of the club.

I handed Sallie a glass of champagne. "Take a swig. It'll make you feel better."

She took a sip and stared off into deep thought. "Major?"

"...Yes."

"Will you ever settle with just one woman?"

"Sure, one day." That's what I hoped anyway. I was on the verge of doing it sooner than later, but I really wasn't sure how soon that would be.

"Do you think I could be that woman you settle down with?"

I searched her eyes to see if she meant it. I found the answer and it caused my heart to skip a few beats. She meant every word she had ever said to me. The bad news was that I was moving to New York, so having a woman was only going to complicate things. If I wanted to get anywhere in my music career, I had to go.

Dodging her question, I responded, "You're a hell of a woman, Sallie. I would be so lucky to have you..."

"But..." She was catching my drift.

"Music can be the only thing I commit myself to right now."

Tears were back in her eyes. It pained my soul because I really wanted to make her mine, but there was no way I wanted to hurt her any more than I already had.

"Sometimes I hate your *music*."

Her bold statement made my blood boil. I was already bothered by Ginger being out with another man and then Sallie questioning me as if I owed her some sort of explanation. They were barking up the wrong tree. "You don't care nothin' 'bout me, then. I ain't none of them cowards like them shines 'round here. I'm gonna tell you like the farmer told the potato – plant you now and dig you later."

I gulped the rest of the champagne that was left in the glass, slapped down money on the table, and got up. I was no longer in the mood to eat and no longer in the mood to sit with her. I got in my car and went over to Bop City. Those damned Alley Cats were there, so I joined their party. That turned into an all night jam session. The asshole in me was a cold piece. I knew I was wrong for just leaving Sallie in the Champagne Supper Club like that, but I went on my way anyway.

Major

"Men have died for this music. You can't get more serious than that." – Dizzy Gillespie

Weeks passed and nothing changed on my dating scene. Sallie and Ginger both felt bad about acting the way they did at the club. They cried, they apologized, and even begged to see me again, but I didn't start back seeing them right away. I played hard to get. Shit, served them right for jumping salty on me.

While Sallie styled Candy Cane, she went on the road with me to Los Angeles, and eventually I got her to spend a few nights with me out of the week. She seemed content with what we had going on.

She rested in the crook of my neck after making love and whispered, "I love you."

Carefully thinking about my response I replied, "I love you, too."

She sat up and stared at me as if she weren't expecting me to say it back. "You do?"

"If I'm lyin', I'm flyin'."

She giggled at my humor. "What made you come to that conclusion?"

"I've been thinkin'." I played with her fingers, intertwined them with mine. "Will you be with me?"

Her smile lit up my dark room and said between kisses, "Yes, yes, yes."

I meant what I said to her and for awhile, she was the only one I was with. Feeling as if my love life was heading in the right direction, I balanced music and Sallie.

Ginger couldn't stand that I chose Sallie, but what else could she do? She had moved on, so why couldn't I? Whenever she saw me out with Sallie, she didn't say a word. Half of the time she was in the company of another man, so she didn't call me or come by.

The Flamingo Club was one of those places that had a hotel upstairs and lots of people occupied their beds after hours. It was owned by Wes, the same guy who owned the Texas Playhouse. I jammed on stage with the fellas while Sallie was home studying for her State Board Exam, and Ginger walked in on the arm of Wes's son, Buster.

When she saw me, she smiled.

I returned the smile and kept playing. I hated to admit it, but oh, she was looking like a fox in that red dress. Old feelings swirled in me. Good cabbage on a silver platter with a piano. Yes, Lawd, seemed like the perfect night for me to commit a sin.

She waited until I was alone at the bar before she approached. "Mind if I join you?"

"Go right ahead. What you drinkin'?"

"Scotch and soda."

"Get the lady a scotch and soda, please."

Immediately, the sexual energy started bouncing between us like a tennis ball in a tennis match. It didn't matter if I was Sallie Aquino's man. Not at that moment. In my eyes, any woman I laid with belonged to me forever. Because of my history with Ginger, I didn't feel guilty about what was going to happen next.

"Where's Buster?" I asked.

As she regarded my hint of vigilance, she smiled. "He went home."

Niyah Moore

"He left you?"

"I told him to. I got a room upstairs... What you think we should do next?" That sly grin was still on her face.

With a smirk, I replied, "Only if you can keep a secret."

"You think I'm a gum beater? Don't worry. Your secret is safe with me."

We finished drinking and I followed her upstairs. As soon as the door was closed, we tore into one another. Clothes were thrown off in a frantic matter. She pulled me to the bed roughly to land on top of her. Entering inside of her love den, I plunged and dug deep. I had a point to prove. She wasn't going anywhere. Thrusting her hips up and rocking to my rhythm, that headboard knocked against the wall.

"Major! Major! Oh, Major!"

The way she sounded when she hollered my name had me rock hard. I flipped her over and pleasured her from behind. We grinded until sweat started to form. Her hands took hold of the comforter and grasped it as tightly as she could. I think she even bit down on a pillow to try to suppress her sounds.

We turned that room upside down, knocked over lamps, knocked pictures off the wall, tussled on the bed until all of the covers fell to the floor, and toppled over the other furniture. Our fuse had been lit and the dynamite finally exploded. Breathless, we lay intertwined. That was one of our most intense sessions.

MAJOR JAZZ

Major

"All a musician can do is to get closer to the sources of nature, and so feel that he is in communion with the natural laws."- John Coltrane

Besides being the ultimate lover, I had too much on my mind and the Big Apple was where I needed to go to be able to record and play on a larger scale. There was so much money to be made there and my palms were itching to grab it. It was time to leave San Francisco and go back to my birthplace to make my music greater. I already did my thing in Los Angeles and recorded numerous records. A lot of opportunity came rolling in, especially from the visiting musicians. Once they heard me at Bop City, they wanted me to play with them in Harlem. My home was the Fillmo' and I loved that place just as much as I loved music, but I could always go back home. I had to conquer my fears and explore other possibilities.

Candy Cane Taylor helped me realize that when she said, *"Fillmore isn't going anywhere. The world needs to see and hear you. If you went to New York, you would definitely make it."*

She was right. I had to leave in order to get anywhere as a musician. Touring was where the real money was. After touring, I was going to be able to come back to San Francisco as a big headliner downtown. That was the ultimate goal.

I hadn't told many about my plan because people always tried to tell me that once I left San Francisco it would be hard to return to the same scene. I didn't want to hear any negativity. I hadn't even told Sallie, which I felt sore about. I was thinking of a way to break the news to her.

Sallie kept asking, "When are you gonna spend more time with me?"

I couldn't spend more time with her. I had to cut ties with her if I wanted my transition to New York to be a smooth one. "I'm working on it, baby." I had to lie. I didn't know what else to say.

Doubt lay in her eyes as well as an ounce of hope. "Well, as long as you try. That's all that matters to me."

I was still working on getting an apartment in New York. I was also helping Frank get into the hospital for drug treatment before the police would try to raid him and haul him off to the clinker. Every time he pawned his horn, it made me blow my top. He was losing everything at light's speed. When his family left, I knew it was the perfect opportunity to do my duty as his friend and help him in every way that I could.

Literally, my hands were full.

I sold every piece of furniture I owned, moved my piano over to my mama's, packed my bags, and planned to air out first thing in the morning. I couldn't stop the word from traveling around as fast as it did. I heard everything from good luck to please don't leave us.

Them damned Alley Cats took me out for drinks at the Long Bar to say goodbye since I didn't want throw a big bash. I wanted to stay low key. I drank soda while they clanked glasses of cognac. They made me wish I hadn't stopped drinking, but I made a promise to Frank. My word with him was solid.

"The 'Mo is gonna miss the most talented pianist in the world," Tyrone declared. "Shit, I'm gonna miss you, Daddy-O. Who else can play like you? Growin' up together created a chemistry that nobody can top."

"You ain't lyin'," I added.

"Nobody can jig like us. Cheers to that." Tyrone lifted his glass.

"You find a place to lay your hat?" Tyrell asked.

"Blue and I found an apartment uptown in Harlem."

"I heard it's happenin' over there," Tyrone said, raising his hand to the bartender for a refill.

"It's happenin'. Y'all should come up that way soon and play. You're too talented to stay in Fillmo'."

They both nodded their heads at the same time.

Tyrell replied, "You may see us up there real soon."

"Real soon," Tyrone said.

"I'll be lookin' for you when that time comes."

"How do Ginger and Sallie feel 'bout the big move?" Tyrone questioned.

"I haven't told Sallie yet and Ginger is masking her true feelings."

They looked at one another with slight frowns. They never liked the way I juggled the two women, but if they were in my shoes, they would understand. Women made it hard for me to be with just one. Like my mama said, I had a cricket's calling song. Once I attracted them, it was hard for them to let go, no matter how badly I treated them.

"That doesn't surprise me that Ginger is hurt," Tyrone stated. "Seem like she's not over losing the baby and all…"

"True…"

"Do you plan on tellin' Sallie?"

MAJOR JAZZ

"I'm gonna call her first thing in the mornin' before I air out."

I watched the two of them get drunk, we reminisced on our childhood for a few more hours, and then parted ways with a bet that they would be in New York in a few short months.

When I left the bar, I picked up Ginger so I could spend one last night with her. It was easier to lay with her. If I would've called Sallie, I would've had to tell her I was leaving. I just wasn't ready to break it to her. We went back to my pad. Ginger lit two candles and turned off all the lights. On top of a blanket on the floor, we made love for the last time. Our kisses held onto the sadness we each felt about not seeing one another again unless she were to come visit me in New York. She was too afraid to fly, so the possibilities of that were slim. She understood why I was moving on. Like I said before, Ginger and I had a bond that no one could ever break.

"I need you to call me once you make it safely. You know how I feel about planes."

"I will."

She kissed the crook of my neck and I felt wetness from her eyes. "I'm tryin' not to get all emotional on you. I can't help but wonder if our baby would've lived if you would still be leavin'…"

I wiped her tears that escaped from underneath her closed eyelids. "I think about her all the time. I think about what she would be doin' right now at this very moment. Whether or not I would still be leavin', I'm not sure, but I do know that this is the perfect time for me to do it."

"I'm so happy you're pursuing what you want," she said. "You deserve to reach your full potential."

"Thank you. Most people don't dig it."

Niyah Moore

"I dig it." She slipped out of my hands and I watched her get dressed. "I'm gonna help you get the rest of this stuff packed up, baby."

"Okay." I stood up on my feet and put on my underwear and pants. I blew out the candles, opened up a window, and folded up the blanket.

Ginger went into the bathroom to freshen up before going to a pile of linen to fold the sheets and towels.

I checked the apartment to make sure I had everything out of the medicine cabinet and from underneath the kitchen sink.

"Where you want me to put these towels?" Ginger asked, folding the last one.

"I have that empty box in the bedroom." I went over to a box and taped it up.

A glass of gin would've been perfect to send me off into the night, but I sipped on water instead.

Suddenly, Sallie walked into the unlocked door without knocking first. She startled me a little because I thought I locked it. If she had walked in moments earlier when I was still beneath Ginger, boy, it would've been a terrible scene.

"Hey," I said, looking and sounding pretty shocked.

"Hello. Did I catch you at a bad time?"

"No... Come on in."

"Is this the box you were talkin' 'bout?" Ginger asked, coming from the bedroom.

With a slight frown, Sallie's eyes darted Ginger's way. Sallie couldn't stand Ginger, especially after the Champagne Supper Club incident, and her mind started immediately running in circles. I didn't have on a shirt. It was lying on the ground next to the candles that still had warm wax in its liquid state. I wasn't sure if she could smell the lingering smell of our sex, but the way she turned up her nose I think she had.

I played the awkward scene cool. "Yeah that's the one. Go on and put those towels in there for me."

Sallie blinked hard for a minute as she watched Ginger pack up the towels.

"What you doin' over here this time of night?" I asked Sallie to find out why she was there unannounced.

"I heard you were leavin'. Were you gonna tell me?"

"I was gonna call you in the mornin'."

Her eyes went back to Ginger. "...Is it alright if I talk to you alone?"

Ginger said, "I was just leavin' anyway." She kissed me on the cheek and gave me a solid hug. "You be safe."

Sallie shifted her weight to her left leg as she watched Ginger leave and close the door behind her. "What's goin' on here, Major?"

"What does it look like?"

"Looks like a whole lot of things you're not tellin' me."

"I'm movin' to New York."

"What's over there in New York?"

"Music... of course..."

Sallie folded her arms across her chest. "Is *she* goin' with you?"

"No."

"When are you leavin'?"

"I'm leavin' in the mornin'."

Sallie's eyes scanned the empty apartment. "Can I go with you?"

"No, you need to be here with your sisters. Sade really needs you right now. How is she holdin' up anyway?"

"She's not dealin' with Jerome's passin' very well, but she's excited 'bout having a baby. It's kind of strange with her and Lu being pregnant at the same time. They really don't need me 'round... I need you..."

"Your sisters wouldn't know what to do if you left."

"I ain't worried about them. I'm worried about what's gonna happen to us when you leave."

"I'm a shoot it to you straight. I don't want you sittin' here waitin' for me 'cause I don't know how long I'm a be gone."

"Seems to me like you've thought about this long and hard. How long have you been planning this?"

"I've been planning for 'bout a month. New York is truly the place for us to thrive right now. Blue just got out of the treatment center and I want to do this while he's clean."

"If I asked you to stay for me, would you?"

Without hesitation, I answered, "No."

"Did *she* ask you to go?"

"Ginger would never go to New York."

"You asked her?" She narrowed her eyes at me before looking back down at the candles and my shirt. I could tell she wanted to say what was truly on her mind, but she knew she couldn't handle it. "I really can't believe you."

Sincerely, I observed her sadness. "Is everything alright?"

She shook her head vigorously. "No, everything isn't alright! You have a funny way of showing me you care. You said you loved me. We're supposed to be together and you still do whatever you want to do. What am I supposed to do without you? Did you ever really love me, Major?"

I took hold of her face with both of my hands, gently, and stared into her watering eyes. "I love you. I really do, but what I'm tryin' to do in New York is detrimental to my career. That's why I can't keep stringin' you along like you're some pull toy."

"You've been stringin' me along like some damned pull toy from the start, so what's the difference?" She rubbed my face with her hands, and tears continued to flow like a rushing river. "Be with me, Major. We can make the perfect family. Let me come to New York with you. Please…" She kissed my cheeks repeatedly.

I wiped her tears with the back of my hand. "Sallie, I can't let you come with me." She sobbed harder. "Listen to me. I know you're hurt. This music runs through my veins and it's deep. You want me to choose. I choose music… I'll always choose music."

Looking up at the ceiling for a brief moment, she replied, "You're the most selfish person I know."

She turned and left. When Sallie walked out of that door, I felt the sharpest pain in my stomach. It was like a tiger was trapped inside, using its sharp claws to dig its way out of me. If I was still drinking, I would've downed the whole bottle to become numb. Being able to feel was a feeling I hated.

Major

"I kept thinking there's bound to be something else? I could hear it sometimes, but I couldn't play it."
– Charlie Parker

Bright lights, city lights... Harlem was at its prime when we moved there. We hit many streets, but you could catch us mostly on 110th, cruising up Lenox Avenue. The Harlem streets had a life of their own, much like the street life we had in Fillmo', and it was hot as July-jam. We played in smoke filled club after smoke filled club seven days a week. I vanished in the music, completely engorged myself, practiced nonstop around the clock, and built a name there. I took a gig at the Cellar, playing the piano with a shining light in the middle of darkness. Frank had gigs all over the place. I met up with him at the after hours eateries and then we would go home.

Twice a week, the only gig we had together was at Minton's Playhouse on 52nd Street. It was a hole in the wall -- nothing fancy at all. Nobody wanted to play in that toilet, but it still paid something. Shit, we were working.

Oh Harlem, the beautiful, the vibrant, the place where bebop had another home. Jazz music was more commercial and celebrated by the masses and it was vivacious. Nothing but good, professional sounds from artists like Louis Armstrong, Duke Ellington, and Dizzy Gillespie came out of New York and I was more than honored to be a part of it.

Frank wound up finding a place for Carra Mae and the kids after a while. He worked like a mad man, stayed away from dope, and spoke of nothing but winning her heart back. It paid off because she and the kids were coming.

I ventured off on my own and made a few new friends here and there. There was this Puerto Rican woman named Tess Ortiz at a Sugar Ray Robinson fight at Madison Square Garden. She was going to her seat a few rows away from the ring, draped down in a white fur coat, matching hat, and scarlet lips. She was on the arm of a rich and cocky Italian man. As she passed me, we made eye contact.

She was breathtakingly stunning. I titled my brim hat and a small sly grin eased one corner of her mouth before she took her eyes off me. The man escorted her to their seats below. Sitting above her, I watched. The fight was exciting, but I couldn't concentrate on what was going on in the ring. I was thinking of a way to talk to her.

After the fight, in the lobby, I didn't have to approach her. She found her way to me, for a brief second. She slid her phone number on small sheet of paper, inconspicuously, into the palm of my hand. Just like that, she was sauntering away, reeling and rocking her hips, before linking arms with her Italian lover. Placing the number in my jacket's pocket, I grinned on the inside.

"I'd walk clear to Diddy-Wah-Diddy to get a chance to speak to a pretty lil' ground-angel like that," Thomas, a new bass player I rolled with, said to me.

"Yeah man, must be a recess in heaven."

I left with Thomas and we got into a cab to head over to an afterhours spot for drinks and dinner. Yeah, I picked up drinking again, but I didn't let it control me.

Niyah Moore

I didn't call her for a few days. I was too busy and sleep was something I needed to catch up on badly. After resting awhile, I found the courage to give her a call. When she heard my voice, she sounded as if she already knew who I was.

"Hello, may I speak to Tess?"

Her accent was strong. "I'm glad you finally called me. I was waiting for you."

"You were waitin' for me?"

"Yes. You're the stranger with the beautiful eyes."

I smiled through the phone. "I didn't get a chance to tell you my name the other night. My name is Major Ingram."

"Well, Major Ingram, I'm glad you called me."

"Would you like to meet me for dinner this evening?"

"I would love to."

She gave me her address and I picked her up. We had a nice dinner over candlelight. I took her home and even though she invited me in, I was the perfect gentleman and declined. On our second date the following week, she invited me in and that time the perfect gentleman inside of me became a new beast before her. Her Spanish-speaking became erratic in a high pitch when I brought her to a climax. It was the sexiest sound.

From then on, she couldn't get enough of me. I gave her the nickname Tesoro, meaning treasure in Spanish. After being around her Puerto Rican family, I picked up a little Spanish here and there. I didn't want her to leave my side or my sight and she preferred it that way. Drawn, purely based on her beauty alone and when she opened up her mouth to speak, her accent drove me wild. I would kill a man with my bare hands for her if I had to. She was that beautiful. We were the envy of every onlooker. Women wanted to be in her place and men couldn't wait for the opportunity just to say hello to her.

I did everything in my power to keep her happy. She craved the finer things in life and I didn't mind providing her with them.

"Papito, I need some more diamonds."

Tesoro spent money as if she needed new things in order to survive. She adored anything fancy and high class. She wouldn't be caught dead messing around with anyone broke and was used to dating men with lots of money. Her taste was on the expensive side, but that wasn't a problem for me. Money came and money went. I just made more, but with the amount she liked to spend, I had to pick up some more gigs. Unfortunately, that meant less time with her.

I bought more diamonds than she could hold and whatever else she asked me for. I took her with me on trips to Canada and then New Orleans. I even went with her to Puerto Rico to visit her family. Her folks were warm and welcoming. I picked up Spanish so well they thought I was from a Latin background.

As soon as we were back in New York, she was sad about going to her place without me.

"Papito, I want to live with you."

I hadn't lived with a woman other than my mother, but it seemed like a good idea when she suggested it. I thought everything in our world was picture perfect until her reality knocked me over the head.

"Why do you always stay out so late? How come you don't like being home? Are you cheating on me?"

I hadn't done anything I wasn't used to doing when she wasn't there.

Niyah Moore

"I'm not cheating on you." That was the honest truth. I had been so blinded by her beauty that no other woman looked good enough to fool around with. "I'm working. Why don't you come down to the clubs to see exactly what it is I do?"

"I'm not going to sit in the jazz clubs with you all night. And do what? Be bored?"

She had been down to the clubs early in our relationship, but frankly, I don't think she ever cared about my music. The fact that I had enough money to quench her luxurious thirst was what kept her around for that long.

"I moved in with you for you. You are supposed to be home. I don't know what this life is."

I paced around the living room, feeling as if I wanted to go get some air so we wouldn't have an argument over something she couldn't control. "Tesoro, please, I had a long night. I'm tired and would like to go to bed. Let's just lay down."

"No! How can I sleep when I can't? How do you expect for me to be your wife, eh?"

"I'm not the marrying type," I answered simply. "So, you don't have to worry about that."

Her mouth dropped open as if she couldn't believe that I would say such a thing. "If you love me like you say you do then you would marry me!" She went off in Spanish rage after that. I could make out a few words hear and there, curse words, but she was talking entirely too fast for me to catch it all. She started packing her things, throwing clothes into her suitcases, still screaming in Spanish. I watched her break my dishes.

I stood there, even moved out of the way, so a few glass pieces wouldn't hit me. A memory of my father beating the life out of my mother flashed before my eyes. That was one thing I was never going to do --

MAJOR JAZZ

hit her. No matter how badly I wanted to, hitting a woman wasn't acceptable in my eyes, especially not when I grew up seeing that in my house. I let her pack the rest of her things and go. Beauty could only go so far because the headache she gave me made me realize I was better off without her.

When Tesoro left, I spent a lot of time alone thinking and drinking. Frank was busy with home life, mostly. That was around the time he and Carra Mae had just gotten married. I went over there from time to time. Carra Mae's delicious southern-inspired, home cooked meals kept me from eating out. Between gigs, she would invite me over to eat with the family. Frank's children were a joy. His son looked just like him and the little girl looked just like Carra Mae. It was funny how genes worked out. Seeing how his family life was at home, made me yearn to start a family of my own.

On the corner of 134th Street and 7th Avenue in central Harlem, I stopped inside of Ray Campanella Choice Wine and Liquors Store to pick up a bottle of gin. I went back to my apartment and sat in the dark, alone. With the volume on low, I played a Dizzy Gillespie record. As I took the first swig straight from the bottle, I got to thinking about the 'Mo. I missed my mother and missed being home period. I wondered about Sallie every day. I wondered if she was married with kids and if she was happy. *Who did she love? Was it still me? Did she miss me as much as I missed her?* Heavy drinking made me think too much. The more I lived in Harlem, the more I realized that I missed San Francisco.

The only light coming through the living room was the red flickering vacancy sign from the hotel across the street. I sat alone in the dark, wishing I had a piano, but one wouldn't fit in that tiny sublet. I could hear a melody in my head. More gin slid down my throat. I wondered if that lonely life was really my life. I didn't think I would miss anything so much. Somewhere in the dark, my lonely soul was waiting for my nightmare of being alone forever to end. I *needed* her. I needed Sallie. I drank more to stop the unwanted tears from falling. How come I hadn't realized how much I loved her before? My thought was to flee from Harlem and make her mine for good.

All alone in the dark...

Panic threatened to break me down, but I resisted. I sat alone in the dark, deep in thought, contemplating my life. Was it always so empty, even with music being my priority? Alone in the dark, Dizzy was playing on that record, bebop. The mystic feel along with darkness held me captive. I suddenly felt scared. Would I be alone for the rest of my life?

I picked up the phone and called Ginger. I needed someone to talk to and she had been such a good friend to me.

"Hello," her raspy voice answered.

It was California bedtime on her end, but I didn't care. I just needed someone to talk to.

"Ginger..."

"Hey, Major... What's the matter?"

"Aw nothing... I just wanted to hear your voice. What's shakin'?"

"Buster proposed... I'm gettin' married."

"Oh? Well, that's good, sweetheart. I wish you the best."

"Why don't you give me a call tomorrow?"

"I will."

"Good night."

I hung up. Ginger and I would always be friends and that's what I loved the most about my relationship with her.

I called Mama, right after getting off the phone with Ginger. When she answered sounding like she was up, I didn't feel so bad about calling so late.

"Hello, Mama. How are you?"

"Cricket, I'm fine. You just gettin' home from a gig or somethin'?"

"Yeah… What's new around there?"

"Things are still changing around here. You wouldn't recognize it if you saw it."

"Is that right?"

"They tore some buildings down. Last week, the whole 1200 block on Fillmore was completely leveled. When you thinking about visiting?"

"I'm thinkin' 'bout comin' back soon, actually. Why are they tearin' the neighborhood up like that again?"

"The Redevelopment Agency is trying to rebuild it up. You know a lot of street fights and prostitution is going on and the police complaining that it's too much crime. The hoodlums are trying to take over things around here."

"Well, the crime rate has gone up a little bit, but so what? They can't do that to us. Is there anything anyone can do to save it?"

"People have been protesting and signing petitions up a storm. We'll see how much good that does. How are things over there?"

"Harlem has been nothin' but nice to me."

"You settle down yet? When are you going to get married? Are you still seeing that Spanish thing?"

"Tess moved out. I don't want to get married any time soon. What's the rush?"

Niyah Moore

"There's no rush. I was just wondering."

"When I do find the right woman, you'll be the very first to know... I'll talk to you later, Mama. I know it's late over there. Good night."

"Good night. I love you."

"I love you, too. Bye."

"Bye, now."

Taking another swig, my homesick feeling kicked in full swing. In the darkness, sly whispers reached my deaf ears. My blinking eyes went to the window. A midnight blue dressed the sky. Something was coming... It was time to go back home.

Major

"I don't know where jazz is going. Maybe it's going to hell. You can't make anything go anywhere. It just happens." – Thelonious Monk

What in the hell happened to the 'Mo?

I didn't think they would get rid of almost sixty square blocks of my beloved neighborhood. The Redevelopment Agency of San Francisco got approved to start tearing down a lot of the businesses and homes while I was away. My return home hadn't been as I imagined. It felt like the air had left me and my caving chest felt a sharp pain every time I looked at the dirt where buildings once stood. The place I grew up, where I started, the place I made my first living playing music, was gone? My heart felt every bit of the agonizing pain like I was having a heart attack.

I stood in front of a demolished plot that once housed my apartment and tried to take the whole scene in. I must admit, it was a lot to comprehend at once. A bulldozer was parked in front of some buildings a little ways down the street. Block by block, everything was completely leveled in preparation for the future of high rise apartment buildings that would give the Fillmore a drastic makeover. I sighed to myself as confusion rose up from inside of me. *Where were the clubs and restaurants? Where were the businesses owned by Japanese, Jewish, and Black people?*

Gone…

When I realized fully that I was still standing in the front of nothing, a tear crept from underneath one of my eyelids. Three years too many had gone by and I felt like I abandoned my home. I left the only place I called home to only return to nothing. Looking up into the overcast gray sky above me, gloom loomed. I walked back to my car slowly, feeling like I was in a live nightmare.

The streets were vacant as I drove and with the sun going down, it looked worse. Barely anyone was out walking around. Where was everyone? Nothing but skeletons of what was once there remained while other properties were boarded up, prepared to be torn down as well. Murky, bleak, and desolate ground went all the way up Fillmore Street unbelievably.

"Jesus," I gasped.

Mama had to move to Potrero Hill because her house was demolished. She was living in affordable housing, although I wasn't sure why she wanted to live in a housing project when I offered to put her in a big house in Oakland. When she refused to move to Oakland, I offered to buy her a house off San Bruno in Hunters Point. She refused to let me buy her a house there. I argued with that woman enough, but her mind had been made up.

She opened up the door with a large grin. "Cricket, I'm so glad you're here. How was the drive?"

I hugged and squeezed her tightly. "It was long; it took four days. I don't ever want to make that drive again."

She guided me to sit down on her shabby, but chic couch. I could tell she upholstered it with some material she purchased. Most likely with money I sent. I looked around, though there wasn't much to look at, and my piano took up most of the living room without a lick of dust on it. Mama never could stand dust.

"Mama, how come you didn't tell me it was that bad over there in the 'Mo? It looks bad."

"There was nothing to tell. I knew you would have to come back and have to see it to believe it. Plus, there isn't anything anyone could do about it, so why have you all worried about it? You've been traveling the world and living your life in New York. I'm so proud of your success. I play your records all the time."

I heard what she was saying, but I was still stuck on how much our neighborhood changed. "Bulldozers destroyed the community and you didn't want to tell me? I can't believe it. What you think they're gonna do now?"

"They say they're going to rebuild it and make it look nice. We can move back when they're done. We all have vouchers to return."

"Shit, do you really think they gonna let us back in after kickin' us out? There's no way. That was their way of getting' rid of us!"

The sound of a child cried from the other room and interrupted our conversation.

"There's a kid in here?"

"Yeah. I got so excited that I forgot she was in here taking a nap."

"When you start babysittin'?" I asked with a frown.

My mother was never the type of mother to babysit anybody's children. I figured in her older age maybe she missed me so much that watching other people's children kept her going.

"I've been babysittin' for a little while now." She nodded before disappearing into the bedroom. I heard her cooing the child before she came out with a

MAJOR JAZZ

toddler girl on her hip. "This is Faith." She sat back down next to me. "Faith, this is my son..."

The child kept her head buried in my mother's shoulder.

"Mama, how long have things on Fillmore Street been like that?"

"Well, let's see, they started tearing a few businesses down right after you left." There was a knock on the door that interrupted her. "Come in."

A woman wearing a white service smock and slacks walked in. "Good evening, Miss Margery."

"Good evening."

The woman paused when she looked at me, her mouth slightly gaped open.

At first I didn't pay her too much attention, but I noticed the air in the room shifted and got thick. We stared at one another for a few more seconds. Then, I realized that the face was familiar. It was Sallie. My heart felt like it stopped beating. She looked good in her beautician work clothes, just as good as the day I left her, only she had gained a few pounds, but not in a bad way. Her slanted eyes and long eyelashes blinked a few times as if she couldn't believe I was there in the flesh.

Mama said to clear the air, "Look who's here, Sallie... my Cricket is finally home."

For some reason she was still frozen. The sight of me had her flustered. I was expecting a hello or some form of acknowledgment, but she asked, "Is my baby ready to go?"

"Let me grab her things from the room." Mama placed the little girl next to me on the couch. "Have a seat, Sallie." She went to the room to gather the child's things.

Sallie refused to sit as if she didn't want to come near me.

Niyah Moore

I decided to break the ice. "Hello, Sallie."

"Hello, Major."

"So, this is your baby? She's cute. How old is she?"

"…She's three and a half…"

My mind didn't take long to do the math. I looked down at the child, who finally stared up at me. She had eyes that were so green. They almost looked blue, much like the eyes I stared at in the mirror every single day. As my chest heaved up and down, I searched for the right way to ask her what was obvious.

Sallie had tears that filled so instantly that they were on the brink of cascading down. "I was tryin' to tell you that night, but you made it painfully clear how important your music is to you. I didn't think you would believe me. I didn't want you to think I was using that to get you to stay with me." Her words gushed out of her as if she had been holding them in for too long.

"Does my mother know?"

"Yes, she knows. I bring Faith over here to spend time with her while I'm at work. I made your mother promise not to tell you. I figured you didn't want to see or hear from me any more."

My Pop may have been a lot of horrible things, but he was there for me when he was alive.

Mama came out slowly. She must've heard what we were talking, but tried to act like she didn't. There was no way she couldn't have in that tiny apartment. "Faith, you ready to leave Grandma?"

I snapped my head at my mother with my throat tightening up on me, making it hard to swallow. "Mama?"

"Cricket, we felt it was best if-"

"*We?* How long have you've known about this?"

MAJOR JAZZ

"Sallie has always been upfront with me. She told me about the pregnancy a few weeks after you left."

"You're my own mother! Why didn't you tell me? I talked to you almost every day while I was away and you didn't mention a thing!"

"Major Ingram, you watch your tone with me." My mama's Jamaican accent only surfaced when she got worked up.

I stormed out of that suddenly too crowded apartment. I needed a place to run off to, but I had no idea where to go. It wasn't like I could run to Bop City and play out my anger. I still didn't know where I was going to stay. I instantly had thoughts of checking into a hotel.

"Major!" Mama called after me from the front door. "You get back in here so we can talk about this."

"I don't want to talk right now, Mama. Just let me deal with this on my own."

"Well, running away isn't going to solve a damned thing. The fact that she's your daughter isn't going to change, especially if your back is turned."

I whirled around and growled at her, "What do you want me to do? I've missed three years of my baby's life 'cause she didn't want to tell me she was pregnant! How am I supposed to react right now?"

My mother had tears in her eyes. I didn't want to walk away, but I was too mad to think rationally. She came to me and put her arms around me. "Calm down, son. I understand that you feel betrayed, hurt, and confused, but look at it this way, you're home now. You can take all the time you need to get to know your daughter... Teach her how to play the piano. She loves music, especially your music."

I took a deep breath to help the smoldering pain leave my chest. She always knew how to throw music

Niyah Moore

into the equation to calm me down. That only worked a little bit. "I came home expecting for it to feel like home. The Fillmo' is gone and I have a baby that I didn't even know 'bout. I just feel like a goddamned foreigner."

"Come back inside, so we can talk about this without the neighbors hearing."

I walked back inside. My heart sped up when I looked at Sallie, who was standing at the door with Faith on her hip.

"Sit at the table, Major and Sallie. We are going to finally hash this out."

We did what we were told. For a moment we were all silent. Mama was waiting for one of us to talk first. She even cleared her throat to hurry us along, but I didn't know what to say to start the conversation. I knew that if I said what I felt, everyone would be mad at me.

Sallie went ahead and said, "Major, I didn't mean to hurt you. I knew this day would come, but I just didn't know when. I should've let your mother be the one to tell you, but she thought it would better if I had this talk with you. Truthfully, I've been too afraid to tell you."

I understood why she was afraid. My moods had been so unpredictable, but for some reason I still felt like that was no excuse. Regardless of my reaction, I still should've been made aware. I would've made different choices for my daughter's sake.

"I would've at least been able to send some money to take care of her if I had known."

"I always gave Sallie what you gave me. She didn't want to take it a lot of times, but I insisted," Mama answered.

"You know my family was doing very well with our cleaning services, but since they knocked our building down, we've been trying to look for a new location to re-open. I've been working at a beauty salon on Third Street to make ends meet."

Feeling troubled, my mind was going crazy. If the clubs were gone, where was I going to play? I was going to have to focus on that another time and focus on what was going on at that moment. There was always the white clubs downtown where I could find another gig.

"I'm sorry for making you feel as if you can't talk to me. I'm also sorry for packing up to leave without tellin' you. That night replays in my head over and over and I should've sat you down and told you the truth. I wish I could change the way it happened."

I wanted to embrace Sallie, but I wasn't sure if that would've been the right time to do it. I missed her more than I thought. There were times when I wanted to write her a letter to tell her how I truly felt about her, but the asshole in me was too selfish to do that one simple thing.

"Major, I knew then why you were leaving. The music that lives inside of you is something that has been with you since you were born. It was wrong of me to make you choose. I don't regret anything and I don't regret having Faith."

Faith was a beautiful, hazel-eyed baby and each time I stared at her, I fell more in love with her. "Can I hold her?"

"You sure can."

I extended my arms and surprisingly, she came to me. I hugged her, kissed both cheeks, and didn't want to take my eyes from hers. All I could do was marvel at her. I longed to know what it was like to see her come into the world, to watch her crawl, talk, and take her first steps. That was something I could never get back.

Niyah Moore

"Can she talk?"

"Yes, she sure can," Mama replied. "That girl talks good."

"She talks too good," Sallie added.

"Do you know who that is, Faith?" Mama asked her, pointing at me.

She shook her head, smiling shyly.

"That's your daddy."

Faith looked at me and her eyebrows nearly connected when a tiny frown formed. I wondered if she really understood what we were trying to tell her. When I smiled at her, she smiled back, making me feel tingly inside.

I looked at Sallie again because it felt so good to see her. Only in my dreams did I see her face and feel my heart skip a beat. To tell the truth, I wasn't just homesick. I missed her the most.

"You married?" I asked.

She shook her head slowly. "No."

I felt relieved that she wasn't. "Me either..." I placed my eyes back on Faith, who seemed to only be interested in looking at me.

"You see your daddy?" Sallie asked her.

Faith smiled and said, "I love you, Daddy." She understood who I was.

Mama said, "We talk about you all the time."

When she wrapped her tiny arms around my neck to hug me, my heart melted. That little girl was going to have me eating out the palm of her hand and I couldn't wait to give her whatever her heart desired.

"Does she like music?" I quizzed.

My mother nodded her head. "She sings and tinkers around on her little piano all the time. I got her one for Christmas."

MAJOR JAZZ

"Well, then, this baby has no choice but to be a musician. Music pumps through her blood."

Sallie said, "She loves music."

"You should see her, Cricket. I play the piano and we sing together every day. I even put on a few of your records and tell her it's you."

I beamed with pride down at her. "Is that right? Well, guess what? Daddy will have to play you a song."

Faith said in her little, sweet voice, "Can you play me a song right now?"

"I sure can, little lady." I took her over to the piano and sat her on my lap.

My mother and Sallie gathered around us. A brand new melody was in my head and I played it, improvising as I went... a song I called Faith. The look on my little girls face as I played reminded me of the same look I had when my father played for me the first time.

Sallie's eyes told me that she was happy I finally knew the truth. I played the song and when I was finished everyone clapped. Faith kept her arms wrapped around me.

Mama asked, "Where you staying, Cricket?"

Shrugging, I replied, "I don't know. I was thinkin' 'bout finding a hotel room for a couple of nights."

"You don't have to go off to find a room. I have a couch right there if you need it."

I took a look at that little shabby piece she called a couch, knowing it was too hard to sleep on.

"Thanks, Mama, but I need somethin' softer."

"You can sleep in my bed then and I'll take the couch."

"I ain't doin' that either. Woman, just let me get a room."

"You stop being so difficult."

Niyah Moore

"How am I being difficult, Mama? I'm not gonna let you sleep on this rock hard couch."

"Well, Faith and I have room over at my place…"

I paused for a second, not expecting that invite.

"You still live with your parents?"

"Heavens no, I had to get my own place 'cause Lu, Johnnie, their two kids, Sade, and lil' Jerome still live there. There just isn't any more room. I'm renting over on the other side of Haight."

The idea of spending the night with Sallie and Faith made me instantly cheer up. "You sure I won't be much trouble?"

"You won't be any trouble at all. It'll be nice having you around for a few days. Plus, I have a nice cozy sofa bed." She smiled.

"Cool."

"Wonderful! It's solved. Will y'all at least stay for dinner? I can whip up somethin' really quick. I have turkey legs I took out this morning 'cause I had a feeling my Cricket was coming today."

"Ooooh, can you use that jerk seasoning and some rice with peas?" I raised my eyebrows. "You got some plantains in there?"

Some good Caribbean food would make me feel like I was truly back home.

With her smile ever widening, she replied before going into the kitchen, "I sure do."

Faith climbed down my leg, went over to a toy box that was in my mother's bedroom, and pulled out a miniature toy piano.

"Look, Daddy," she said. "I have a piano, too."

I spun around on the piano bench to watch her. "Look at that lil' lady. You gonna play somethin' special for Daddy?"

MAJOR JAZZ

She nodded and went to town on that little thing and all I could do was smile proudly.

Sallie sat next to me on the piano bench. "I'm so happy you're home. I thought I would never see you again."

"It's funny 'cause I was startin' to think the same thing, but I'm glad I'm here. I'm still in love with you. It never went away."

She dropped her head bashfully. "Really?"

I inched in for a kiss. She didn't budge. When my lips touched hers, it felt like magic. "I love you more than you know. I had a lot of alone time to think about you. This time I know what to do to take care of you. I love you."

"You don't know how long I've waited to hear you say that."

I nearly swallowed her tongue, but she stopped me from getting too carried away.

"You sure you want me on that sofa bed, tonight?" I asked.

She giggled. "If I let you into my bed, Major, we may end up with baby number two."

"What's wrong with that?"

"You must be here to stay…"

"I'm not going anywhere. I'm here to stay."

We were silent as we stared at one another for a few seconds.

"So, how's that drawbridge? Any boats passin'?"

Again, she giggled as if I were tickling her. My suggestion of her moral turpitude made her that way. "You're still nasty as ever."

"That'll never change... You still haven't answered the question."

"I guess you'll find out when we get *home*."

"Home… I like the sound of that."

Niyah Moore

PEACE IN THE STORM PUBLISHING, LLC IS THE
WINNER OF THE 2009 & 2010 & 2011 AFRICAN
AMERICAN LITERARY AWARD FOR
INDEPENDENT PUBLISHER OF THE YEAR.

WWW.PEACEINTHESTORMPUBLISHING.COM

Meet Niyah Moore

Natural talent shines brightly through the words of a writer with a desire to share a gift with the world. Born and raised in Sacramento, California, Niyah Moore was touched at an early age with the precious gem of prose. At the age of nine years old, she participated in a Writer's Workshop and displayed a special knack for writing that sparked a flame for a romance between Niyah and storytelling. Just like any loving relationship, Niyah's love affair with words began to bear fruit. Before she finished high school, she had completed five novels, wrote three school plays, and had written a play for her church. No small task for someone in middle school; yet she pulled it off with ease. A childhood hobby begged for legs of its own as she matured into an adult. Niyah listened to her calling, finding the time to write in the mornings while raising her family. Under the subtle pushing and guidance of a literary mentor who was well known in the literary industry, Niyah decided to pursue a career in writing professionally. She submitted a short story to the *Mocha Chocolate* anthology in 2008 and was accepted as a contributing author. Inclusion in that literary work gave her the courage to submit to various others and a literary journey for her began to take form.

One leap of faith jumped into several acknowledgments of talent. Her works include novels, *Guilty Pleasures* and *Bittersweet Exes*; and inclusions in several Award-Winning and Award-Nominated anthologies such as: the 2012 AALAS nominated anthology *Heat of the Night*, 2008 African American Literary Award Winning Erotic Anthology, *Mocha Chocolate: Taste a Piece of Ecstasy* Anthology; *Chocolate Historie D'Amour* Anthology; *Souls of My Young Sisters* Anthology and *Mocha Chocolate Remix: Escapades of Passion*. Niyah's short story "After Dark" will be included in the anthology, *Zane presents: Chocolate Flava 4* releasing in the Summer of 2013. She is also one of the contributing author duets to the groundbreaking anthology, *Pillow Talk in the Heat of the Night* which will be released in the Spring of 2013 as well.

Niyah is a mother of two, who loves sharing her love for words with the world and who looks forward to the publication of her new novel, *Major Jazz*, which is scheduled for release under her new publisher, the Award-Winning Independent Publisher of the year, Peace In The Storm Publishing.

Childhood dreams and real-life talent are the foundation to making Niyah Moore, Literary Phenom, what she is today.

You can find more information on Niyah at www.niyahmoore.com.

Niyah Moore

CPSIA information can be obtained at www.ICGtesting.com
Printed in the USA
LVOW071533290313

326724LV00002B/213/P